GHOSTLYFE

Mark Laxton

Preface

One of my favorite movies is, The Prestige. The movie starts,

"**Every great magic trick consists of three parts or acts.** The first part is called "The Pledge". **The magician shows you something ordinary**: a deck of cards, a bird or a man. He shows you this object. Perhaps he asks you to inspect it to see if it is indeed real, unaltered, normal. But of course...it probably isn't. The second act is called "The Turn". **The magician takes the ordinary something and makes it do something extraordinary.** Now you're looking for the secret... but you won't find it, because of course you're not really looking. You don't really want to know. You want to be fooled. But you wouldn't clap yet. Because making something disappear isn't enough; you have to bring it back. **That's why every magic trick has a third act, the hardest part, the part we call "The Prestige"**

My life, and the three parts of my book are inspired by this structure.

There's a scene where Christian Bale's character and Hugh Jackman's, are to try to detect a magician's method for a trick. An elderly Chinaman makes a large fish bowl appear from no-where full of water with a goldfish. They watch him as he walks stooped over half crippled to his carriage. Christian Bale's character points out that the man walking crippled is the act. That he carries the bowl between his legs and covers his method by acting crippled. As they go back and forth, he says, "This is the trick, this is the performance, right here. This is, why no one can detect his method... Total devotion to his art, a lot of self-sacrifice. You know? That's the only way to escape, all this. Ya know?"

"Total devotion to his art, a lot of self-sacrifice"

This is a line that has stuck with me since the first time watching this movie. I have adopted it, as a governing philosophy in my life! This book is meant to help everyone who reads it find the ability within themselves to change their lives and create the life they've always wanted. It is an account of personal experience and growth through trials, emotions, and road blocks that have been overcome in the pursuit of success. We all have a different definition of success and the only input I have there is, always strive for your greatest definition! While the trials and circumstances I share may be nothing like those you face, the crippling emotions evoked are exactly the same. Humans are humans the world around. Different experiences, languages, cultures, but the emotions, actions and psychology behind them are the same. I share my experience as real and raw as I can so that we can relate. It is not a "feel good" book or something to feel sad for or be amazed about. It's simply me sharing my experience the purest way I can, in an effort to help ignite the fire of ambition that burns within each and everyone of us! That my words and the truth behind them will be felt to the depth of the soul. To inspire the slightest action toward the change we all wish for. Growth, change, success, and improvement are muscles. Mental muscles that when exercised, strengthen, the more reps we do the stronger we get. This has been my experience. The books, processes, strategies, and techniques are habits I've practiced and built up over the last 10 years. As an individual takes actions (big or small) they build strength and momentum for more action and growth. This book is written in a way that is meant to showcase the action required in the face of great resistance to succeed. There are many experiences left out. There are many influential people in my life that have taught me very valuable lessons. Nothing is forgotten, I draw strength from any and all energies I have ever been blessed with.

I use every experience to better understand myself and more importantly to fuel the pursuit of my purpose. Anybody that isn't mentioned in this book, believe me you all play very important roles in my life! It is because of all my experiences, that the books I've read have been able to affect my life the way they have. Thank you! The knowledge learned and applied is simple and can be learned and practiced by all. Purpose has been my greatest helper along the way. I mention a counselor multiple times in this book. This lady seemed to me, to be the first to believe in, and fight for me in a long time. When my fire was nearly out, she helped re-ignite my flame of ambition and purpose years ago and inspired me to become my best self. Since working with her I have taken on the life purpose of igniting that flame within us all, the same way she did, to the masses! This is the first book in a series of books that will release every 5-years!

Read this and say, "this is amazing because I can do it too!"

Enjoy

Section 1: Lose

Chapter 1

July 22nd 2011. I crouched over my best friend thinking I'd protect him if the Driver of the car tried to run him over again. Seconds before that, I watched from 10 feet away as the driver ran Scotty down, intentionally running him over. Hitting him with the front bumper, turning the car and accelerating. I watched as Scotty was twisted, whipped, then sucked under the tire, pinched between the car frame and asphalt, rolling him until the back tire bounced into the air off his body.

Scotty Ford was pronounced dead just a few hours later.

I knew he was dead on the scene after the initial contact of the car violently whipped his head to the ground. Denial immediately kicked in and convinced me he'd be fine… Deep down I knew he was gone.

The next two years was an accelerated downward spiral into a deep dark hole that had already been dug deep. At that time in my life, I was drinking alcohol and smoking weed every single day and had been for about 5 ½ years. I had a pattern: 7 months on opiates (while still drinking and smoking), then five months without opiates.

Before Scotty died, I was already a blackout drinker and an overdose user. I pushed limits passed the edge and for some reason was always pulled back up the cliff by some safety line I can't explain in any other way than the power of The Universe or my Higher Power saving me.

My downward spiral really took its turn at the age of 17, as a senior playing in a JV football game and taking the field for the last time. I was lost. The only thing that was important to me was over. Football completely consumed my life from 6th grade until Senior year. It was all I cared about, even though I only started a few of the years I played. It was life.

I didn't party much at all up to that point. The night football ended, I was drunk. I was then on the substance abuse fast track! Within 6 months I had tried almost all substances. I was drinking, and smoking weed every day. OxyContin was being used more and more frequently. I would mix Ecstasy, Xanax, Weed, Oxy, and anything else that might be floating around.

In August of 2006, after graduating, I moved down to St. George Utah to start the semester at Dixie State University. I was down there for 5 months and was able to stay substance-free for 4 of those months. I withdrew from school within the first 2 weeks.

A couple months before moving I had a pretty serious longboard crash. I was knocked out and woke up on my hands and knees with my hands in my own throw-up. My friends said I rolled 20 feet or so... out cold, seizuring, throwing up, and seizuring again. I went to the hospital, they told me to take it easy. Physically, mentally, "just take everything easy."

Well as you might guess, I kept partying and partied even harder! They gave me painkillers that were great to snort! Anyway, I was on repeat. I'd tell a story then turn around and tell you the exact same story again without realizing. For about 7 months after the accident, I had Post Concussive Syndrome. Anytime I went from sitting or lying down and got up too fast, everything would spin. This was my main reason for withdrawing from school. That and the financial aid that I got approved for only covering $400.00 per semester. I withdrew within the first 2 weeks of my first semester, never to return to college.

I lived in St. George for 5 months and really enjoyed my time down there. I was bussing tables at Outback Steakhouse for 3 months, then started framing houses for the last 2. I had some experience framing houses before. Working with my brother for a few months before I went down to St. George.

I moved back to Orem and was immediately drinking, and smoking weed every day again. I was also using OxyContin as often as possible. My opiate use was steadily increasing, and I was eating Ecstasy multiple times a week. I had a good hook and good buyers, so I would supply, make money, and have some extra pills to eat free every time I would middle man a deal.

Bringing this full circle, I was always a daily user of alcohol and or drugs. From day to day alcohol and weed were a constant and any other drugs were used whenever they were around. Which was quite frequent. The only two things that changed along my path was the amounts of substances and the daily use of opiates. I recall a time a few years into my partying, waking up on a friend's couch, urgently searching for weed, alcohol, anything to alter my mind. There was nothing anywhere. I was frantic and the friends I was with had not a care in the world to find alcohol or weed. I remember this day very clearly. It was the day I realized I was an alcoholic, that drugs and alcohol had become a necessity, not just a good time anymore. Realizing this, I did nothing to stop or slow it. I just did my best to enjoy some good times along the way. I most certainly had some great times!... I also created quite the path of destruction, heartache, trouble, and pain. Putting myself in situations and scenarios that should have killed me many times over. But, by The Universe's grace, I am alive, strengthened infinitely by my past.

My choices brought trials, like watching a kid who wouldn't fight his own fight, jump in a car, run over, and kill my best friend. I've been arrested 3 times and put in jail once. I've been to court countless times. Hurt friends, family, and myself. Been through two rehabs, lived in a sober living house twice. Blacked out from drinking and overdosed from shooting heroin countless times. Been jumped, beaten up, fired from a door to door sales job! Who gets fired from a door to door sales job? How? I tried to quit using and drinking so many times I had given up on it being a possibility. Probation multiple times didn't slow me down. Two ambulance rides as the result of heroin overdose happening within 5 weeks of each other didn't even make me flinch.

Chapter 2

On November 3rd, 2012, I had been using heroin, smoking weed, drinking, eating muscle relaxers, and snorting Xanax. It was my good friend Miah's birthday weekend and VIP was reserved at a nightclub for him. Full bottle service and not too many people drinking meant that I had more than my fair share of alcohol. I left the club around midnight with my brother because we wanted to go get high. We picked up some heroin then parked on the side of our parent's house. We both shot up and my brother went into the house to hide his needle and spoon before he drove me to my apartment.

I knew from the second my shot hit that with everything in my system, I had too much! I could taste the heroin in my tongue, I had been here before! I was going out as I watched my brother walk in front of the truck...

The next time I was conscious, I woke up to a blue screen lighting the place and reflecting on diamond plate. Two men in blue button-up shirts moving about. I remember thinking, 'fuck I'm in an ambulance.' The next thought was, 'this is going to be an expensive ride.' Immediately after those thoughts, I began to vomit uncontrollably, yelling at the EMT's to, "fucking un-strap me!" repeating this in between exorcist vomiting! All they said was, "turn your head to the side."

My brother was already at the hospital when we arrived. He was much more traumatized than I was.

He told me he was freaking out, shaking me, slapping me! Gave me mouth to mouth, doing anything and everything he could think of to get me to wake up. He said I was completely white, and my lips were purple. He didn't notice I was gone until he made a turn while driving and I just fell over on the seat. Thank God he called 911 when he did! He watched the paramedics shoot Narcan into my body. Narcan blocks the opioid receptors and reverses an overdose. He watched them cut my shirt (one of Scotty's that was very special to me, I was pissed while I was throwing up in the ambulance and realized it was ruined) and use a defibrillator to shock me back from a flatline. Yes, by the time they arrived on the scene I was technically dead, no heartbeat. My brother watched every second of it frantically wondering if he had just watched his brother's last moments.

Being wheeled into the hospital and seeing my brother scared and pale as if he had just seen a ghost threw me off. I was freezing cold and yelling at the nurses to, "get me more fucking blankets!" Again, on repeat, they told me I had so many on me that more wouldn't do anything to help. I just kept yelling for more blankets because I was fucking freezing! The energy was so frantic, so spacey, and tense. Yet outside of my chattering cold body I was calm, collected, and fine. Looking back on it, it's kind of eerie how unphased I was. Soon, I was warm and making jokes about the whole thing. Nobody else saw any humor in the situation.

A lady came in and read off the drugs that were in my blood. Heroin, THC, Benzos, some sort of muscle relaxer, and cocaine. The only part that was a surprise was "cocaine," I wasn't alarmed though (I Just didn't remember doing cocaine recently enough for it to be in my system). I just asked when I could leave. The nurse told me that one of the numbers on the monitor had to stay above 90 for 5 minutes before I could go. I put all my mind's concentration on my breathing and keeping that number above 90. I was out of there within 10 minutes.

My brother told me told me how horrible that was to watch and how scared he was. I just shrugged it off. As far as I was concerned, I simply took a nap and was totally fine. This is how I've always reacted to everything in life, no matter how fucked up I felt it was, or how shitty things were.

While driving home at 4 am, I called my dealer and lined up the pickup of more heroin. When I hung up the phone, my brothers only words were, "you're a fucking idiot." I told him I wasn't going to use it until tomorrow, he just needed to pick it up. I made him commit to picking it up after he dropped me off at my apartment. I woke up around 2 pm, went into the kitchen and started talking to my roommate in the living room. I literally felt like I had been hit by a train, my roommate asked why I sounded like shit. "You sounded fine yesterday." I showed him the bracelet on my wrist and nonchalantly told him about my overdose. He expressed concern and care that I barely responded to because my brother was downstairs to pick me up.

I could finally get high again!

My brother commented to the fact that I still smelled like throw up and he couldn't believe I hadn't showered. I only cared about one thing, getting high. It's a very fucked up space to be in. Knowing that the only thing that makes you feel okay in life is the very thing that killed you the night before. I remember asking my brother if the Narcan and everything from the night before got me past withdrawal symptoms. I paused while looking at my shot of heroin ready to go, thought about quitting, then shot up anyway!

Chapter 3

Nearly 4 weeks later, I was flying to Galveston, TX to board a cruise ship headed to Jamaica, The Cayman Islands, and Cozumel, Mexico. It was an incentive I earned selling alarms the summer of 2012 in Alabama.

That summer was one of the hardest things I've ever endured. Scotty and I did everything together, every summer. Being out selling alarms the summer after Scotty died, the way he died, was pure hell. Everything I did, big or small reminded me of Scotty. For the first summer of my door knocking career, I was having OxyContin shipped to me while I was out there. I have never wanted to quit or give up on anything more than that summer in Alabama.

I began going through withdrawals in Texas. I cold turkey quit pretty much every time I left the state of Utah. Especially for anything that had to do with alarms. I withdrawal differently than most people.

When I withdrawal, I must be active, I must stay occupied. Working or playing, alcohol and smoking weed as much as possible is a must. For these reasons, nobody ever believed I was going through withdrawals while I was. How could they? They have no idea what's going on in my head, what it takes to quiet my mind, or how impossible it is to shut it down completely.

For example, that first night in Texas when the beginning of the intense withdrawals started. I recall clear as this moment, sitting with 3 others in a hotel bathroom smoking a blunt with the shower running. We all had our conversations going and a good high kicking in. Then, with no warning a screeching, top of the lung, ear-wrenching scream drowned out all the all noise for at least 15 seconds! That is a long time to scream! I looked at the walls around the bathroom, the other 3 people, the steam and smoke. Lastly, I stared at myself in the mirror and realized nobody else skipped a beat. They heard nothing. I concluded it was all in my head. This is a small example of my overactive brain. I used substances to the extreme degree. I've described attempting to silence my mind. I'd use anything I could to do my best to quiet the brain. There is no silence.

This cycle of 7 months of opiates and heavy drug use then 5 months of alcohol and weed went on for 3 of the 7 years I consistently partied. The last 14-month runner began in Alabama April 2012 and ended June 13th, 2013. 5 weeks after my first ambulance ride. The day I returned from that cruise, I took my second ambulance ride.

This was the beginning of the end, even though I had a very long way to go. Not only was I a far way off, but the path ahead of me was a ridiculous obstacle course with plenty of twists, turns, and hurdles. I'd argue that's how life is for everybody. Life is a test, we have to prove ourselves, we have to show that in the face of insurmountable obstacles we can find a way to win! As individual's life's situations and circumstances are different but the feelings and emotions are the exact same.

That second ambulance ride set forces in motion that I do my best to explain. My Higher Power gave me so many gifts. This one though, I was not going to let anything keep me from taking full advantage of! Not even myself.

Oh, and if this intro has been confusing, scattered, looping, hard to follow, or chaotic... welcome to a glimpse of my mind, get ready!

Section 2: Experience

Chapter 4

My first rehab was at the Renaissance Ranch in Bluffdale, UT. I checked in at the end of November 2011 for a 60 day in house treatment. My family set up an intake interview without me knowing. I had an incident while in Texas on a sales trip selling alarms door-to-door. The first night I drank myself into a blackout and pissed all over a new, high profile recruit's luggage. The next day, went into a co-worker's hotel room while housekeeping was in there and stole some of his alcohol. I was fired and sent home early.

Fired! From a door to door sales job! I called my mom and told her I needed help with my addictions. I had a plan to get my mind straight and just needed a little help. Without my knowing my family set me up.

My little brother picked me up from there airport and drove me straight to an inpatient rehab intake interview. I felt betrayed, I was furious! I didn't like how they did me, didn't like it at all. After the intake interview, I was given an ultimatum without an ultimatum, whatever that is?

After resisting going in for a few days, I finally gave in and took the opportunity to improve my life. On the way up to check in, I made my dad stop by a friend's house so I could smoke some weed before checking in. He walked in while I was hitting the pipe, the look on his face just showed disappointment.

I completed that 60-day rehab, then moved into a sober-living house that was suggested by the rehab. The second day out, I had a drug test as part of the rehab's continued program. I tested positive for THC, 61 days after I last smoked! They said it was impossible for me to test positive after that long and didn't believe I hadn't smoked. The only way I'd be allowed to move into the sober-living house was to go to a detox for 3 days. Yes! I was forced to go through detox for, WEED, I smoked 61 days prior!

I started a car sales job, which I had to drug test for. I passed. Finally, people believed I didn't smoke. I only lived in sober-living for 7 weeks on that go around.

My mom was the one that found me and called the ambulance the second time. I did my best to sweep that first one under the rug, very few people knew about it, Miah and a few others. All that knew expressed sincere concern. I, of course, disregarded it and told them they were overreacting. While at the hospital the second time it all came out in its severity. The paramedics and nurses remembered me and made sure they spoke of how bad that first ride was. Stating with the details of having to be shocked back to life from a flatline status. Even though my mom did the best thing she could when she found me, she didn't like the way the paramedics handled the situation and was upset that they forced me to go in the ambulance. Before the paramedics put me on a stretcher or anything,

I had woken up on the ground in my parent's house and was coherent. They would not treat me there or let me stay at the house.

While lying in the hospital bed talking with my parent's, they mentioned that they had dinner with one of my dad's mission companions. Rod Jepson owner and operator of, at the time, Arch counseling. They later changed their name to Suncrest Counseling, but it was all the same. Same counselors, same model. A full-service therapy and addiction recovery center. Within a few days, I met with an LDS ward bishop to see if the church would pay to put my brother and me through Arch's Intensive Out-Patient (IOP) addiction recovery program. Both our parents, my brother, and I were there. At the end, the bishop concluded that our situation and circumstances warranted help and they'd do what they could to give us a fighting chance by paying for us to go through this program.

My intake interview happened to be with an attractive counselor. She asked if I was military and was a little surprised when I told her no. She asked, "Why are you here? What are you wanting to accomplish?" My response, "I want to get clean and sober and be able to have an occasional drink."

"We can help you do that." She asked what was going on and why I was overdosing. As I told her my story, I mainly focused on Scotty and the trauma there. After hearing that, she said she asked military because she could tell there was PTSD I was dealing with.

I continued on. I told her that I was to the point that, "I don't care about anything. I just don't give a fuck! The only thing that I'm fighting for, the only reason I'm here... is that I will not let my story end the same way it has for so many from Utah county that, I lost my battle to addiction! My obituary will not state, he's returned to his father in heaven after years of struggling with addiction and now he is at peace." I will not let my story end like that!

Chapter 5

For the first couple of months of the IOP, I was in there between 30-40 hours per week! Doing 1-on-1 counseling, group therapy, neuro-therapy, and activity therapy. Pretty much every single day I'd leave treatment and go get high. I rarely ever lied about it when I'd return to treatment the next day. I was told that I was defeating the purpose of coming if I kept getting high. That I was keeping myself from making any progress by doing so. My response, "I'll stop getting high when I'm good and ready and not until then." I would drink and use heroin during this time.

I got a part-time job making $9.00 an hour, so then I was going to my IOP 20 hours per week. Outside of work and treatment I would journal, draw, color, and meditate. All with the purpose of improving myself. I was keeping a dream journal, writing out, drawing, searching the meaning of my dreams. I would do exercises like journal questions written with my right hand(dominant), then answer those questions writing with my left hand. This exercise is supposed to help you respond with the subconscious mind. The theory behind it is that by using your nondominant hand you're being vulnerable. It helps access a childlike state or reveal the subconscious. There are several studies that go into detail about it, but this exercise helps us access parts of the brain we don't often use. Giving incite to underlying beliefs that are manifesting themselves in our behaviors.

None of this was easy and really. I didn't want to do any of it. The cold truth, the force that would not let me rest, was, I was fighting to stay alive! I had hit a point with my using that I learned about in my first rehab but did not think was real, "reverse tolerance."

It says that the body can hit a stage with your drug of choice where the tolerance you've built up *actually regresses*. I have experienced this. I got to the point where even if I shot up half my normal shot, (half of a balloon) I was going out (passing out, hitting the floor etc.) Shoot up and wake up however long after not knowing what happened or how long I'd been out. This was happening while I was alone and was the same thing that happened that night my mom called the ambulance. It was at this point I started taking "drug addict safety measures." I was smoking my heroin instead of shooting it up. I would go a couple days without using every-once in-a-while but would drink myself into oblivion and physical pain. It was during this time I realized all substances were the exact same for me. Nicotine, heroin, and everything in between. I was all or nothing with no middle ground. Anything that would alter the way I felt I would use as much as was available to me.

This is months of work. Months of counseling and groups. Journaling, drawing, processing, and dreaming! Scratching, clawing, fighting forward inch by inch! There were plenty of times I was going through withdrawals, hungover, exhausted, to the point that I didn't even get up and go to treatment. Plenty of days that I would sleep in and miss half of what I was scheduled for. More importantly, there were more days that I felt as shitty or shittier than I just described, and I was able to drag my ass in for the full day!

I do know this, it was much easier to get up and go no matter what, when that attractive counselor was first on my schedule. I also stopped scheduling early morning sessions altogether because I would rarely wake up for them. Unless that was the only time I could see my favorite counselors. The neuroscience specialist was also attractive and super awesome! So, If I had to go early morning to see either of them I would make it happen.

I was smoking heroin or drinking almost every day still, but at this point, I was reading, writing, drawing, journaling, and improving. I still had to trick myself into doing all these things. I was so used to doing what I wanted no matter what. Changing those habits and behaviors was very difficult work.

I started framing houses again and was working at least 32 hours a week, taking off Thursdays to go to treatment for 8 hours. For me, getting high and scraping by was comfortable. It was easy and I was used to it. Turning my life around was very uncomfortable and a lot of hard work. Emotions are no joke, digging into the past is not something that can be taken lightly. I needed to pay close attention to the details and the seemingly small things that were ruling my life. Pushing through a lot of pain, opening-up being very vulnerable repeatedly, it was just shitty! I put myself in a fucked-up place though, and I had to work my way out. The more I could take responsibility for everything in my life, the quicker my progress came. It was like I was eliminating excuses from my mind and receiving more solutions to problems as a result.

In my opinion, living a life centered on getting high and dragging that out is much worse than a quick death. I was exhausted by all the work I had done, and even more drained when I thought about how much more work had to be done. I remember one of my sessions, the counselor had me sketch with colored pencils. No agenda, or assignment, just sketch/color.

While we were talking, she told a story that I have never forgotten. "When hiking the K2, the second highest peak in the world, The Sherpas or guides tell the hikers: "Never ever look at the peak, focus on your feet and when times get tough keep telling yourself: Just one more step, just one more step." That lesson has stayed with me. I've repeated those words many times when I wanted to quit climbing mountains, literal and metaphorical.

In-the midst of all the inner turmoil, I was constantly being told that all the work I was doing was being negated by the fact that I was still getting high and numbing out. Rightfully so, I understand where my counselors were coming from! They just had no experience with one key element!... You can never count Mark Laxton out!

Chapter 6

This IOP process started December 18th, 2012 and continued intensively until June 13th, 2013. That's the time frame of my most intensive work with the counselors/programs offered by Suncrest Counseling. During this time of intense work digging into my past, looking closely at how it affected my habits and behaviors created a lot of change. I numbed the emotions with drugs and alcohol to dull the pains I was facing head on.

Even still, this work resulted in yelling, screaming, fighting, crying, loving, hugging, and understanding. Any human emotion you've felt or can think of is included on my list. Physically fighting family and friends, malicious verbal attacks on friends and family. Malicious verbal, mental, and emotional attacks on myself! My journal from this time period is ruthless, majority of it is directed at myself! There was also a lot of growth, forgiveness, love, care, and help! A lot of healing came out of all the nastiness. Beautiful!

I remember mid-May 2013 writing in my journal that I'd be living in Salt Lake City within 3 weeks. Had no idea where, why, who with, or how at the time. I just remember writing it with a very strong conviction. I then followed that up with speaking it out loud to the people who were around me.

Near the end of May, I went on a father-son campout. It wasn't something I wanted to do, I had just been developing the habit of doing things I didn't want to. Mainly because not many of the things I wanted to do were any good for me! The bishop who okayed the funding for my treatment was there, and we had a good talk about life and how everything was going. I was able to spend quality time with my dad, speak about some heavy things, and hike with him to enjoy the sunrise. All in all, it was a good weekend especially considering I was going through mild withdrawals. I was excited to get back home so I could get high and feel better though.

Throughout April and May, I had been communicating through Facebook with an old roommate from the sober living house I stayed at after my first rehab. He had moved back to the sober living house and was the house manager. He told me I should find a way to move in asap a room just opened-up. I called my bishop and explained I felt the next step was to make this leap and asked him for help with the first month and a half rent. Told him I'd find a way to take care of the rest after that. Arrangements were made and I moved in June 13th, 2013 with $5.00 to my name, no job, no food, and scared shitless! I got high the morning on my way to the sober living house knowing that was the last time, and it was time to withdrawal again. In the beginning, to financially survive my friend loaned me $80.00 and I earned a little money taxiing people around in my car.

I had 1 week of mild prescriptions to calm my withdrawals. I was restless, exhausted, and very anxious that first week. During which I read the book The Soul's Code, In Search Of Character And Calling by James Hillman. Beautiful book! It helps put meaning to any and all circumstances, traumas, and experiences we've had throughout our life. It and journaling really helped my mind come out of the heroin fog. In that first week, there was a day that everything in me was wanting to pickup some heroin and get high. A girl I had worked with in the past hit me up and wanted to hang out. She was my saving grace and kept me from going downtown to get high!

My path hasn't been pretty, and it definitely hasn't been easy. At times it's been plain old ugly. There's been plenty of times I wished I could just give up! Things that I've said and actions I've taken that have hurt others for life. I've caused fights and worse yet, damaged emotions. Humans being raw, real, and vulnerable equals a beautiful, painful mess! That's life. As humans we do our best, unfortunately, a lot of time our best is kind of shitty. The good news is that if we continue pushing for self-improvement and are willing to persist and endure, the rewards we receive are better than we can imagine!

Chapter 7

This leap into the sober-living house along with continued work, sponsorship, meditation, and counseling, graced me with the strength and ability to stay clean and sober from all substances minus nicotine for 7 ½ months!

My counselors were baffled and mind-blown. A couple of them stated, "It's amazing! It's like you just magically flipped a switch! How did you do it?"

These statements and this question pissed me off! It was disrespectful to me! There was no magic, no switch was flipped! I drug my ass to that treatment center day after day, counselor to counselor, group to group, activity to activity, month after month! In-spite of, feeling like shit, not wanting to go, wanting to give up. Still getting high for a long enough time while in treatment that doubt was creeping in and whispering, "You're lying to yourself, you're not going to quit using." These counselors watched this shit first hand!

Read my journals, studied my drawings, interpreted documented dreams, suggested books to read, loaned me books. Dissected, critiqued, suggested, encouraged. I followed all of it whether I wanted to or not!

There was no magic, no fucking magic switch! Just down and dirty persistent work!

All of this came together at the perfect timing and I was able to hold it together for just long enough. December 2013 was when they finally followed through with the trial for Jeycob England, the boy who ran over and killed Scotty. It had been pushed back multiple times over the previous two years. There was controversy over the fact that he had been "out on bail" the entire time leading up to the trial. Bail that was denied by two judges and only approved by a 3rd judge that allegedly had a family connection to Jeycob's father.

There was some "hot shot" lawyer that took his defense pro bono, knowing that it was going to be a high-profile case. It definitely was, everybody in MS knew the story well before it went to trial.

No matter how much preparation was done, once actually there at the trial, preparing to take the stand, then taking the stand was beyond nerve racking! Emotions were very intense, and everybody was on edge! The defense attorney only asked me a few questions, then was done with me. He had me get up and describe how Scotty was run over. Then he asked what way the car left the parking lot. Their entire defense was that it was all an accident on the way out of the parking lot, that he didn't purposely run Scotty over.

I responded, "I didn't see where the car went, I was crouched over my best friend who had just been run over, protecting him, thinking he was going to be run over again." He asked the question again, I repeated my answer! It went much worse with the other witnesses in our group, so I heard. As I listened to the defense attorney's closing argument, I couldn't keep from going fire red! He was twisting my words, adding to them, taking away from, I was furious! I had to head to the airport after hearing that and wonder what the verdict was going to be.

6 hours later, on the layover in Texas we received the news, Jeycob England was sentenced to 20 years in prison found guilty of manslaughter. There was finally closure to the entire ordeal.

Chapter 8

From November 27th, 2011 until present day Alcoholics Anonymous and its 12 steps has had the biggest positive impact on me being able to stay clean and sober. Having over 39 months clean and sober today (Sep. 2nd, 2018) is the result of me adopting the 12 steps of AA into my life as a governing lifestyle.

Make no mistake, it's taken a lot of trial and error. Countless books, numbers of counselors and sponsors. 4 relapses preceded by time periods of being clean and sober, deteriorating to destruction, construction, demolition, and a lot more construction. With help from any place I could pull it from. Today I can look back on nearly 8 years of work improving myself. Using every interaction as a mirror. Making mistakes, hurting friends, family, loved ones, and associates. Running from mirrors and life. Reaping havoc on people, places and things just because I didn't understand myself. Bringing myself to the end of my rope and finally planting my feet and facing the destruction I caused. Ready to square up and fight my way to a better ME, a better way, and a better life!

The 5-month drinking 7-month opiate pattern carried a theme over to my pursuits of a new lifestyle. I would go 5-7 months clean and sober then fall off for some time. I had a 4-month drinking binge from September 2014 until December 2014. By the end of it, I had started using opiates and muscle relaxers. That's when I put a screeching halt to it. I always went back to AA when I needed to get sober because it works, every time. No matter what without fail it is a successful method to get clean and sober.

Self-help books – law of attraction/hermetics Divine Magic by Doreen Virtue, As A Man Thinketh by James Allen. I have listened to As A Man Thinketh close to 1,000 times. I time my workouts to it and have listened to it almost every time I've worked out for over 2 years. Poverty to Power, as well as psychology and neuroscience books like Blink by Malcolm Gladwell, RAPT Attention and the Focused Life by Winifred Gallagher. Inspirational books like The Slight Edge by Jeff Olsen, Uncommon by Tony Dungy, The 4 Agreements. Just to name a few. Books have always played a huge role in my progress! I had a 14-month stretch where I would read at least 10 pages every night. Books are my favorite method for growth.

I've also done spiritual workshops and seminars. Fire-walks, ropes courses, meditation, prayer, journaling, and deep introspection. GOD campouts, recovery conventions, and a lot of service. Talks with addicts and alcoholics, making coffee or meetings, chaired meetings. Working through issues with a sponsor, anything staying sober requires. Whatever it takes to make it through tough times. During all this, I was able to hold a corporate job for 2 years! I never thought I'd hold any job that long. Especially a corporate one.

I learned how important it is to set goals. Even while living at a sober living house, working with a sponsor, and seeing a counselor once a week. I still had times I would become overwhelmed and resort to some kind of substance to relieve the pressure of life. The first time, at 7 ½ months it was a cough and cold medicine. Clearly, that wasn't anything like alcohol or heroin, but I used much more than the suggested serving to numb out and relieve my stress. It was the same for me as drugs or alcohol. Same actions for the same desired effect. The second time was alcohol for 4 months, ending with pills. The third time was heroin for a weekend, kratom for 1 week, and wine on that last day May 26th, 2015. That's the last day I put any mind-altering substance in my body other than seldom nicotine until July 31st, 2016.

One of the most important lessons in life came during this mayhem. I had a couple things happen that placed me with a temporary manager at work. This manager felt high amounts of stress and strain from being responsible for two teams and having to deal with 3 new very loud personalities coming from one team. Not knowing how to handle us, she took time out of her day to teach us about the importance of goal setting and the huge role it played in her success. Yes, she was very successful! She spoke about her goals to own real estate, multiple houses. Her goals and reasons for travel. Then she showed us her stats and what she'd accomplished in pursuit of those goals! Dominant performances against collection targets. Number 1 on the floor hitting 200 and 300% of goals 13 months running, until getting promoted to manager. That lesson stuck with me and changed my life. I started setting and writing out goals and it changed my life overnight.

Denis Waitley, Best-selling author, motivational speaker, and consultant, in my opinion, says it best:

*"**Goals provide the energy source that powers our lives. One of the best ways we can get the most from the energy we have is to focus it. That is what goals can do for us; concentrate our energy**"*

As simple as this statement is, it has had a life-changing effect on me. My largest goal in life is to turn GHOSTLYFE into a universal symbol of inspiration! That goal is followed closely by my goal of owning and operating multiple Alpaca Farms using the raw fleece to create peacoats, overcoats, hats, scarfs, and gloves. Branded as Royalpaca, inspired by GHOSTLYFE with locations all over the globe starting in Ireland.

These goals have grown in clarity and size over the years. The first goal was as simple as "Alpaca Farm," "Georgia." Since those goals were set April 2014, I have never failed to hit at least 100% of a work target when I maintained discipline and focused on keeping a strong structure. If one of the three was missing, then I didn't come close to my targets or goals. Before understanding this, I was always between 70-80% of target. Once I had it all in place, I went 16 months straight hitting or exceeding 100% of goal, 1st place in floor wide competition one year and 2nd place the next. On weekends and days off I would go to alpaca seminars and study alpaca to learn what it takes to be successful. I've volunteered on a sheer day to help shear a heard. I worked for people with success in marketing so I could successfully market my ideas and products when the time comes. I moved to Georgia at the end of May 2017. 3 years after setting the goal. It took longer than I planned, and I don't have an alpaca farm yet but by the end of 2019, I will!

Around the same time I was setting the Georgia Alpaca Farm goal, I said I would live in Ireland in the next 3-5 years. That was May 2014. Today is January 4th, 2019 and I am writing this from the Westbury Hotel in Dublin, Ireland. Things change and sometimes things get pushed back. Part of this trip is to get an idea of what has to be done to move here and start a business here. My recently written goals aim to live here by 2023. I'm pushing to make that happen sooner than later though.

The year 2014 was, in hindsight a breakthrough year for me. With goals set, my work ethic increased. I was reading anything that could help me increase my abilities and improve my skills.

The Slight Edge, by Jeff Olson has been one of the most influential books! This book was suggested to me by a lifelong friend, Brad

Lunt. Brad and I have maintained some sort of communication our entire lives. Even when I would disappear because of my drug use, we never missed a beat reconnecting. Now a days, we speak every couple of weeks about business, life and growth. We help each other to stay accountable and bounce ideas back and forth. This relationship has been very helpful to my life and my success in numerous ways!

The Slight Edge teaches of compound interest but in-regards to the daily habits we practice. Encouraging the reader to make smaller daily goals as opposed to bigger, less frequent goals. Making sure we do those positive actions every day to build momentum and confidence. That over the years with consistency and commitment your efforts will compound and skyrocket you into levels of success you couldn't even imagine before! I have watched the results of this philosophy and practice affect my life and it has been astonishing.

Not to say there haven't been setbacks, delays, traumas, and difficulties. Life is always going to do its best to knock you down. If my book teaches anything, hopefully, it will be that we have the strength and ability within ourselves to overcome the most catastrophic horrors imaginable. With relative ease, contrary to what we often believe or have been told.

The principals taught in The Slight Edge helped me to get a promotion at work and utilize my time outside of work to add more productive learning actions to my life. Giving me the opportunity to practice and improve my sales skills while learning basic effective practices for marketing and advertising products. Simply by showing up to help with any opportunity offered.

Chapter 9

I was helping a friend run booths selling screen printed shirts which was practice for my sales while being able to see how to market well. This was a goal I had written in my journal 1 ½ years before. I planned on doing it much sooner, but it was awesome to see it come to fruition even after I had forgotten about it.

People around me took notice of the momentum I was building, it was during this time GHOSTLYFE was created. A co-worker and I would continually brainstorm ideas. We decided to move forward with an inspirational clothing line "GHOSTLYFE" an acronym. For me, it stands for Get High On Success Today Love Your Fight Everyday. For my business partner, Go Hard Or Stop Trying Live Your Fears Everyday. For him, it was a reminder to overcome and accomplish the tasks he feared doing, the things he knew would improve his life. For me, it is a reminder of the addiction I had overcome. That my life used to be about simply getting high and nothing else. That there were plenty of days during that period of my life where I didn't want to fight at all. Taking that desire to get high on substances and replacing it with success and successful actions. Falling in love with self-improvement and progress, fighting daily to ensure I locked these habits in as a lifestyle. Turning the process into my drug!

www.ghostlyfe.com, www.myghostlyfe.com I have blogs and you're able to comment!

The symbol represents the success pyramid (The model for success that UCLA legendary coach John Wooden created) surrounded by the ghost tail. To represent making it your own. No one person's path to success is going to look the same, the principals used to achieve success are, however. This is the reason for the acronyms combined with the symbol. It's meant to inspire, to remind everyone that success is a lot simpler than we often tell ourselves. That developing simple daily habits and taking these actions in-spite of all the shit life throws at us will create success! Using these actions to make us successful in accomplishing each-and-every goal we set for ourselves. We would never expect to be able to dump a puzzle out of its box and have it fall into its completed placement. Goals are the same as puzzles, regardless of the difficulty level and the size. It's going to take time, effort, and thought to successfully complete.

GHOSTLYFE almost immediately took on a new meaning for me. It wasn't something I wanted to monetize. I don't believe we should HAVE to pay money to be inspired. Not that there aren't many inspiring things I'd pay plenty of money to see. I just want to gift anybody and everybody, regardless of how little they have with inspiration. Inspiration is the gust of wind we need in moments of fear, or disappointment, during the times that our motivation falters and we want to give up. One of my favorite quotes is "Motivation will die, let discipline take its place" -Tom Crean, Georgia Bulldog's head basketball coach.

There will be days when no amount of motivation or inspiration will get us moving. It seems like in these moments, the more responsibilities we have, or even just think about, the more it cripples us. At that point, the only chance we have depends on our discipline. How good are your "go to" habits? What have you trained yourself to do when you want to give up? Have you practiced successful actions enough that they are on auto pilot and they take over? "Amateurs Practice Until They Get It Right; Professionals

Practice Until They Can't Get It Wrong" - Unknown

"You're not going to work to become a motivational speaker and not get paid for it, get fucking real with yourself!" -Satema Gali

GHOSTLYFE? How do you go about creating a universal symbol of inspiration, a life's work without monetizing it? Simple really, keeping my purpose in mind, every single action I take creates a ripple in the universe bringing myself and my purpose closer together! Action produces a result, and in my experience, positive constructive actions bring my goal to me! Another very influential work I've read is Ralph Waldo Emerson's, Compensation. You can google it or, the book, Ralph Waldo Emerson's Essays and Poems is like $6.00 and has a, large number of his works including, Compensation.

Influenced by this theory, I've found that taking positive, constructive action regardless of the situation or circumstance produces positive results connected directly to my end goal. Surprisingly, even if and especially when I neglect my own tasks to help someone advance themselves in any way. Things would seem to magically happen for me, bringing my goals closer to me. The most important factor to this, in my experience is keeping a laser focus on the goal. This concept is still mind-blowing to me but has proven to be true every time.

At this point in my life, my direct aim and purpose is to turn GHOSTLYFE into a universal symbol of inspiration. That is my lifelong goal, my legacy. Every goal I accomplish, every experience I have, is with the purpose to build up my platform, to extend my reach and influence to accomplish this goal. Being in Scotland on the island of Yell is to give myself a good chance of seeing the Northern Lights (bucket list item) and cut out all distractions to write this book.

We all have bucket list items or things we want to do. This book's only purpose is to help everyone to believe, not only that are we capable of experiencing everything great we desire, but we truly deserve these things! As we accomplish our positive goals, and express a constant gratitude to a Higher Power, we are gifted energy to continue to aim higher and accomplish bigger!

Not to say we won't experience setbacks, mistakes, or sometimes outright failures. Of course, we always have many of these feelings. There will be fears, doubts, discouragements, and the urge to give up. The depth of these emotions is equal to the height of the goal. As we continue to push forward in-spite of it all, as we find a way to make the best of any and every situation no matter how grim or stark it may appear, we build momentum, confidence, and conviction! We learn how to do whatever it takes to succeed and use every single experience to benefit us and propel us toward our goal!

Throughout your journey from day to day, you're going to have successes and failures. Even if you're only successful at one thing within a day, you can use that as a positive point of reference. You can then begin to add more actions to the success column using the same process you used for that one successful act. Improvement is the key and nothing else.

Chapter 10

August of 2016, I had recently broken up with my ex-fiancé and watched myself and my successful actions deteriorate. I tried with everything I had to continue my successful actions, but I allowed my circumstances, thoughts, feelings, and emotions to drag me down and deteriorate down to failure. I was going to bed late, sleeping in until 1 or 2 pm, working very little, and I regressed to where I was mentally weak again. I had not locked in discipline, was surviving on inspiration and motivation. When those died so did my success. Every day the battle that consumed my mind was that I was better off drinking and using drugs. Because at least if I had an addiction to support, I would get my ass up and work every day.

At that time, I was living in a friend's unfinished basement and earning just barely enough to pay my most important bills but neglect the rest. I used the excuse that my sleeping habits were so bad only because I lived at a house where everybody was partying until 3-4am 3-4 times a week. Now, this has some effect on my sleeping habits, yes, but I am a firm believer that your external circumstance simply reflects your internal condition.

Keeping this in mind as much as possible I was able to calm myself as frustrations bubbled up due to the chaos surrounding me. I would disappear to the basement, write, meditate, and dissect the thoughts, feelings, and actions going on within, throughout, and around. Taking these actions while the music was blasting, and everyone was partying loudly. I would do my best to read and write so I could put purpose and meaning to everything going on in and around me. Even still there were a few times that I blew up and yelled my frustrations about the noise, partying, and mayhem. More often when they'd party, I would pack a bag and pillow and go stay at my exes or my parents just to find comfort in something familiar and get a good night's rest.

With all the craziness around me and boiling up inside me, I was in a space where my sobriety was in danger. Having the goal of staying sober and improving my recovery for the rest of my life, combined with living the steps in my daily life long enough, gave me the awareness to know I needed to be taking a lot of action to outweigh the turmoil and stay sober.

I was going to a meeting every Tuesday night. I would get there early usually and be of service by setting up chairs or helping make coffee. I was approached by someone who asked if I could take over their service position and be responsible for making the coffee for everyone each week. It was a 4-week commitment but the first week was that day, so 3 more weeks. I agreed to take over, then after the fact, I was told there was a follow up part to the commitment. After the rest of the

3 weeks, the person making the coffee becomes the chairman of the meeting for 4 weeks. Conducting, leading and guiding the meeting. I was asked again if now knowing all of it I would still take the service position. I still agreed. Any reluctance I had in my head was outweighed by my commitment to staying sober and knowing these service positions were positive actions that would aid the achievement of that goal made it easy for me to say yes.

A very important event took place, even though my roommates and friends at the house were partying all the time. We still had times where we would come together to share ideas, thoughts, goals, dreams, and ambitions. We would sit down with notebooks, brainstorm, and challenge one another. Write down our fears, write out our failures, and share it all out loud. Just recalling these sessions to write about them now makes me emotional. We would share our

WHY… our biggest goals our greatest dreams! Then we would write out and talk about everything we were doing that kept us from getting closer to our goals. We would talk about roadblocks, hurdles, difficulties. Then we would take responsibility for habits and actions we'd repeat that kept us from, and sometimes moved us further away from our goals.

One night in-particular stands out to me, the challenge was to write down our successes and failures. My list of failures at the time was too long to count: relationships, financial responsibilities, sleeping habits, working/producing daily, reading daily, the list went on and on. To the point I stopped. Struggling, I asked myself: What was a success at that point in my life?

After some time, I was finally able to write, being clean and sober. Sometime after that, my fitness. That night, staring at that paper, seeing only two lines with anything written in my success column, feeling the weight of all my failures, I became overwhelmed. It shifted! That space broke. I knew that staying clean and sober was the most difficult task I had accomplished. I remembered how many times I had failed at it before (4 times stretched over 4 ½ years) I remembered my previous longest length of sobriety was just shy of 7 ½ months. I also found strength in the fact that I had made it through many more difficulties this time around. I was never able to stay sober through anything like that before.

That night, approaching 15 months clean and sober, I could see so clearly what it took to get there. I could see the nearly 5 ½ years of years of work and improvement. I Had the clarity of the changed actions to make it past my previous road block. The biggest change I made to get that length of sobriety, aside from goal setting was step 8 and 9 of the AA

12 steps. I had relapsed 4 times on step 8. Finally, I passed it.

I wrote a list of all I had harmed and made amends to them all. I was too prideful before. Between step 9 and a spiritual seminar I did. That seminar's follow up assignment was to "clean up messes" aka make amends. I made amends for more than 90 days straight! This changed my behaviors when I wronged someone and my life. I knew everything in my failure's column could eventually be moved over into my success column! Sobriety was in my failure column multiple times and for good amounts of time. Seeing it in my success column in the mix of all the shit I was walking through helped me realize I had everything I needed to be successful and it was time to get to work!

Chapter 11

I had been selling credit card processing since December of 2015. There were some good months, but I wasn't making enough to survive. Me being the way I am, I could not give it up because that would require admitting failure. Outside of running appointments and cold calling B2B, I would do anything I could to earn money. Usually, I'd help my brother build houses, or finish and remodel basements in the evenings and on weekends.

I had walked away from two books of business that I built up. They weren't much but the residual from them would have covered the finances I couldn't pay easily. I was building my 3rd book of business this time entirely on my own and had a couple great months in the past enticing me to stick with it.

Seeing very minimal success and lacking any motivation to work, I applied for a job waiting tables so I could earn while building up a new merchant services book of business. The person who interviewed me explained it rarely goes well hiring a person straight on as a server without experience. However, she did hire me on the spot for a position as a busboy.

Right about this time I moved into my life long friend's house, Nick Harding. A block away from the restaurant I just got hired at. I was running merchant service cold calls and appointments, bussing tables at night, and helping my brother build when I could. Along with all of that, I would find opportunities to go run sales booths with friends that had their own companies. If there was a chance for me to practice and improve my sales skills I was there!

During one of my good months with credit card processing I bought Grant Cardone's "Close The Sale" app, a $100 app with sales theories, techniques, closes, and sales videos. Anytime I was in a social situation I didn't care for, I was studying the content of that app!

Once everything was in place and my life had structure again, it started to improve quickly! Even though it was hectic and very busy, it calmed. I was reading consistently again. My reflection and introspection produced ah-ha moments that helped me to improve my work and production mentality. I realized I had a lifelong theme of working 6-7 months then easing up or stopping entirely.

The most influential factor in this habit was 4 consecutive summers knocking doors selling alarms. Working with plenty of people who were successful enough in the summer to be able to work very minimally the rest of the year. I was not this successful at summer sales but acted as if I was successful enough to live that lifestyle. I did this at the financial expense of those closest to me. I would go earn, spend fast, be broke, and rely on my ability to convince others to help me with promises to pay them back at certain times. Sometimes my deadlines were met, and sometimes they weren't. For the most part friends and family were almost always paid back, just much later than promised, leaving those people in stressful financial situations due to my lack of financial ability. Even after identifying and acknowledging how my lacking the ability to be self-supporting was negatively affecting those around me, It was still years before I was able to truly be self-sustaining and self-supporting.

I was trying to learn from the actions of the people who were successful in the areas I wanted success. A very dear friend Jai De Jong, a man I look up to who has always been very helpful to anything progressing my life is one of these people. I met him through a longtime friend and my AA sponsor at the time. One night at the gym I was telling Jai the entire story of my credit card processing journey. The ins-and-outs, the potential the industry has, and the position I was in at the time. We discussed him helping me out by letting me use a cubical that was available on his sales floor, having me come in and develop a sales script with his help and guidance.

I have never been more insecure than I was when I walked onto that sales floor. My sales confidence was at an all-time low. It had been a couple months since I had closed any deals. Every person on Jai's floor was a shark! Trained, practiced, developed, disciplined, professional salesmen! It was intimidating and exhilarating!

For about 2 weeks I went in there and made calls. Some days I was there the entire day and others just ½ day, depending on my schedule at the restaurant. Jai and the others on the floor would give me tips on calls and help me structure a good sales script. They sold online businesses and consulting for those businesses.

I took home one of their sales scripts to study it, so I could call on some of their leads to try to earn some money and more importantly, get a feel for a successfully structured script. I had a voice recorder that I would record my calls with so I could listen to myself.

One particular call, a lady hung up on me, I asked Jai why she hung up at that point in the call? He wasn't sure because he couldn't hear her. Once I listened to the recording the question changed to, why didn't she hang up earlier? I sounded horrible, my tone was flat, and my confidence was so low I couldn't understand why anyone stayed on the line with me for longer than a few words. Jai would listen in and tell me what to say and how to say it when I had someone stay on the line.

I hated it! I would walk into the other room because my sales insecurities didn't want to hear all the things I was doing wrong. I was too prideful to admit my sales confidence was so low. After the first couple weeks, I stopped making calls altogether. I started listening to everyone on the floor pitch, I would listen to the closers close! They had a phone system where I could listen in and hear both parties live. It was beautiful! I was envious. I wanted the skills and abilities they had!

I would go into the office, study sales material, and listen to these guys in action. Jordan Belfort's straight-line persuasion segment on tonality was Jai's first suggestion. I listened to it 3 times while studying the guys on the floor. The next suggestion was, You Can't Teach A Kid To Ride A Bike At A Seminar by David H. Sandler. In my opinion, the greatest sales work ever published/created! Jai had told me to read it two years before. In hindsight, oh how I wish I would have!

Even still, it was a thing of beauty. Because I was working nights and weekends at the restaurant, I had the opportunity to use any free time to read this book. Then, in the mornings and on my days off, go in and listen to a sales floor that lived the teachings, techniques, and processes of this book! For 6 weeks I was able to read, observe, and study the greatest sales philosophy I've come across yet!

While studying and growing during this time, I looked at the reality of my situation and put the facts of my 13 months of credit card processing in front of me. I started the merchant services industry to earn enough money and build a residual that would afford me the freedom financially, and time-wise to be able to pursue GHOSTLYFE and start my Alpaca Farm. In 13 months of selling credit card processing, I had made just over $20,000.00! No wonder I was in debt, stressing about money, and having to rely on others help to survive. My continual choice to pursue that romanticized idea cost everyone around me. My lack of acknowledgment and refusal to take responsibility put those close to me into similar stress because of my reliance on them.

Back at the time, I moved out of Shawn Greenland's basement into Nick Harding's house. As I was moving out, I took a big pickle jar that we used to make cold brew coffee with. Shawn said, "Georgie, what ya doin'?" I told him, "taking the pickle jar" and left. He didn't get much further with me to question it or anything. I was gone too quick. He still makes fun of me and we still laugh about it, the way he sat there in disbelief and wonder as to why I just stole his pickle jar!

I had a plan, I had seen it in my head for some time. I took it home and with a black sharpie wrote, "Georgia Jar" on it. All the money I got went into it. Every penny and anytime I had to pay for anything I had to take away from the Georgia goal. It forced me to be mindful of how I spent (a first for the nearly 29-year-old me). It always kept every action focused on the goal. It was and still is, "my manifestation jar" that jar has taught me

a lot and helped me manifest as well.

Chapter 12

Once I finally gave up credit card processing, my energy for life came back instantly. One description of depression that always stuck with me is, "depression is simply turning down the wrong path, then continuing down that path." That has always been the best description of depression for me. I like it because it's simple and keeping it simple, makes it easier to make your way out of the depression. The longer we continue down the wrong path, the deeper the depression and the more catastrophic the event that turns us around needs to be.

In my experience the turning point is the scariest part because you know how far you've gone and as shitty as the depression is, it's comfortable and known. Turning around and deciding to get out of the depression means venturing through the unknown, which is extremely uncomfortable and down-right terrifying. It is very difficult to see this scenario any other way. But making a comeback out of a depression is just like anything else in life. The more we do it the better we get at it. As we continue living, we start to notice when we've made a wrong turn sooner. We also discover that the lessons we've learned while on the wrong path are very helpful to our comeback, as well as very valuable sometime in the future! Any lesson learned can always produce a positive result in the future. It is up to us to see this is true.

With my energy restored I was bussing tables at night, framing houses with my brother, sometimes before going into bus tables, and doing everything I could to improve myself and my life. While studying sales materials the number one thing preached across any and all sales material is, practice, practice, practice!

My friend Rob Molling, owner of 1% Fitness which is a complete meal prep service company came to mind. I love their food, their service, and everything they do. I had been a paying customer of their services before but wasn't able to afford the plan I wanted out of pocket at the time.

Rob's a long-time family friend, he grew up in the in the same county I did, and we all knew each other decently well. I had some rare free time one morning and decided to ride the bus up the canyon for fun and see the snowy mountain canyon views. As I was letting my mind wander, enjoying the bus ride, I decided to convince Rob to let me run booths for 1% Fitness in exchange for food. He told me he had just brought on two more brand ambassadors and didn't really need another. I responded with, "yeah but I'm not an ambassador, I'm a straight mother fucking hustler and you're never too full to not need a good salesman." With that, preparations were made to have me start running booths on Tuesdays and Thursdays! I now had filled my free time with a way to practice the sales techniques I had been studying while receiving good healthy food for my services! Rob also surprised me when he let me know I was going to earn $20.00 per person I signed up. This created a huge positive swing in my finances! Not spending money on food and earning while practicing sales. This was one of the best moves I've made in my life!

That was January 2017. I quickly took on more responsibility with 1% Fitness. I was writing sales scripts and doing anything I could to help. I blocked out my schedule Tuesday and Thursday. After running my booth each of those days, I would work around the kitchen making calls and doing anything I could to get more new customers. Equaling anywhere from 10-14 hours those days. Outside of that, I was either bussing at the restaurant, framing houses, or spending my little bits of free time with my favorite people, Dom and Suraya.

Dom and I met November 2014 while working together at Credit Corp, the debt collection company. Our interaction slowly increased, training, questions, emails, then dates. We laughed a lot and were both driven to accomplish more and be better. We are wild and silly, adventurous, and spontaneous. We hit it off from the start. She would always tell me about her daughter Suraya. Told me she was something special and that maybe one day we would meet. I remember Dom preparing me, "she's very independent and doesn't open up to many people," "she's pretty shy and don't take it personally." Suraya was almost 5 years old when I met her. I remember meeting that little ball of light, her huge energy is something I can't describe or do justice! We connected on a deep and profound level immediately! Dom was shocked, she couldn't believe what she was witnessing, so confused. We were running around yelling, screaming, playing tag, and hide and seek. Making jokes about mommy and each other, I was throwing her up in the air. We were laughing and connecting in a way her mom had never seen Suraya connect with anyone before! I remember sitting back and watching her run around, wondering who she was, how we were connected, and how many past lives we had lived through together. It was something else!

Suraya, Dom, and I would use every second we got together! Adventuring anytime we could! We'd go hiking, out to eat, to the park, anything we could be "wild and crazy" and loud doing! Suraya, ever since I first met her when I asked her what she wants to do her most common response is, "I wanna run and scream and be wild and crazy!"

Staying super busy and picking up work any time I had available was the norm. As we were nearing the end of our lease at the apartment, everything in life was settling a bit. One day Dom looked me in the eyes and said, "let's get you to Georgia." That stands out to me as one of the most important things anybody has ever said to me! Dom has always been 100% supportive of whatever I've had going on in life and that's why we still communicate to this day. Regardless of what we've done to each other or what issues we have we have always supported each other in every way we could. No matter what. Our relationship is a beautiful evolution of human growth and understanding, in-spite of mistakes and downfalls.

All efforts were already for Georgia but having a partner that is 100% supportive in such a way just kicked it into overdrive! Working doubles was my standard, framing, boothing 1%, selling at the kitchen, doubles at the restaurant! I was earning money from everything I did, and it was paying off. The Georgia Jar was being added to by myself and Dom. I was working so much that months went on that I put off an entire day date I promised Dom. Every time I had a day off, I'd pick up work between one of the three gigs I had going. This, of course, created some frustration and finally, I did leave an entire open day for us.

Dom and I are silly, goofy, loud, and crazy! We love deeply and are both very passionate about life! We are caring, very intelligent, and insanely intuitive. The levels our conversations reach are only surpassed by the love that we share. The energies we exchange across the board are on a cosmic level! Our date day was beautiful because of the way we had been working we were truly able to enjoy it. All of our responsibilities were taken care of and we had enough money that nothing was a stress.

Writing this in this moment, it stands out to me that I work so hard and push the ways I do to create just that! The ability to truly and completely, stress-free, enjoy that day off. That vacation, the expensive meal, the show, or expensive clothes. It's so simple but just stands out, how great a gift it is to be able to experience these things without the financial stress that so often troubles the back of the mind.

In the mix of all this, I went through the training to become a server at the restaurant. It was a pay cut for me, but I knew it would be benefit us moving to Georgia and easily getting a serving job down there.

Chapter 13

Within the first week of becoming a server I had a very scary experience. While driving home from the restaurant one night, there were cars stopped and people out of them. Running and waiving down the freeway. Following the cars and people waiving I pulled to the right and slowed way down. Going about 5 mph, trying to figure out what was going on. To the left, there were shoes laying on the road, and further up a man, visibly road rashed, his pants down past his waist. Him lying there exposed and lifeless. I knew right away he was dead. Getting home I couldn't keep my mind from flashing between that image and Scotty. So similar, so surreal, yet all real as anything could be.

I looked up the news story and confirmed what I knew. The news story said he was on a motorcycle with no helmet or protective gear, lost control, and was dead on the scene. This had me reeling, back and forth between Scotty and this man I never knew but carried the same heavy heart for him, his family, friends, and loved ones. All I could do to lessen the weight was write something. Which I did and posted it on Facebook.

https://www.facebook.com/mark.laxton.5 /posts/1414696895220136:0

All I could think of was how fragile life is, how important it is to milk every second you get and make the absolute best of it. Make sure the ones you love know it. The entire event had me shook, it scared me, I didn't want to leave the house. The thought of what if that was the last time, I'd hold Dom or kiss Suraya goodnight as she slept? These thoughts had me stuck for hours!

Even when I woke up and went to work, my mind was still stuck in that PTSD flashback! Scotty, the man on the road, the similarities. Thoughts, feelings, emotions! I wanted to cry and breakdown. At work I made mistakes and the General Manager jokingly asked, "what the hell is wrong with you!?" It took everything in me to not break into tears in front of everybody. I had a family date that evening that I wanted with every part of my being to cancel. I was scared shitless, wanted to curl into the fetal position, cry, and sleep forever! I thought I might sink back down past the depth of my previous worst depression. The one I sunk into after watching Scotty die the way he did. It had taken me nearly 6 years to get my life in order the way it was. This one event threatened all that work and had me fearing it was all going to be unraveled!

I knew I had given my word to Dom and Suraya, so I made sure I followed through with that. Dom knew I was in a bad space but had no clue how to help. Suraya thought it was weird that I wasn't giving her the attention I usually did, but she wasn't discouraged from making sure she got it! I did my best to interact and laugh, to be fun for her, but I was really struggling. I felt like an empty shell lost in the heartbreak of mortality. Suraya was her excited, energetic, amazing self, "Hey Mark!" she seemed to be repeating all night. At least that's what I recall the most. We were swimming in the pool, sitting in the hot tub the three of us, just having a relaxing night. Suraya was making crazy faces, one of our favorite things to do back and forth! Splashing me, throwing stuff at me, "Hey Mark!" Anything she could do to get my attention.

It was about 3 hours into family date night, "Hey Mark!" I looked at her it clicked! My soul rejoined my shell and the crippling fear had gone! God bless that little child and her energetic persistence. She brought me back, she pulled me out of the zombie-like PTSD flashback I was so frightened and scared of. We enjoyed a good family night, playing, swimming, laughing! That little girl still has no idea what she did for me that simple evening.

Minus the couple mistakes I made and wanting to cry during my morning shift I made it through that one without missing a beat. Within 24 hours Sunday night through Monday evening. It's a great example to me of how we can magnify and amplify things in our heads so easily. We can cripple ourselves. All it takes is for us to allow our momentum to be stopped or decide we can quit or take a break. If we do take a break or quit for a second, we may keep ourselves from the simple breakthrough that gives us a new burst of energy! We never know where it's going to come from, in this case, it was a beautiful little energetic girl.

The Friday of that same week I was driving home, something in my head (The Universe) told me, "you're about to get a sign" Almost instantly I received a text from Trent Hatch, "bro call me ASAP, Miah" I called him and in so many words he was trying to tell Miah was dead!

I couldn't believe it. Miah and I spoke a couple times a week every week. He was doing pretty good at the time. I asked how? Trent said they're pretty sure overdose. As shocking as it was, it wasn't as much of a surprise as you might think. Definitely heartbreaking, though. I remember thinking what a fucking idiot, immediately after that thought, was I've done much stupider and much worse in larger amounts. For some reason, I'm here and he's gone.

Again, the massage milk every second, make the most of yourself, love the ones close to you as much as possible! The second time this week I received this message. I remember thinking Miah's heart was done, he just wanted peace, wanted it to be over, for the fight to finish. His heart and mind just went peacefully. At least that's what I had to tell myself to be able to charge on and press forward.

Repeat of Monday, Friday night shift, busy weird headspace, made a mistake. The GM talking shit, asking, "what the fuck!?" a good friend, in recovery, and manager at the same restaurant. Told me to follow him, we went into the hall. I told him about Miah, he knew about Monday, he asked, "can you work, or do you want to go home?" I Paused... "I got this, I want to work." I walked in, prepped the drink order I had already taken for my table of 7, turned in a way that one cup with mountain dew in it tipped and spilled off the tray. I caught it with my left hand, turned, refilled it, placed it back on the tray. Then went and did great the rest of the shift!

As get-togethers for Miah's passing happened, conversations about it with more people happened. I realized I had become a machine to death. Miah is a great friend of mine, we maintained a friendship since I was 15. That's more than 14 years of ups and downs of friendship and life. He's the one who accepted my addiction in such a way it inspired me to change. He asked my help in his own battle with drugs and alcohol.

Something he didn't talk about with many people. I sometimes ask myself to this day, if I did enough to help him.

Him being dead due to overdose makes it easy for me to think about the "what if's?" the same kind of "what if's" I can so easily run through with Scotty. Miah was there for me a lot of the time when I needed him. I tried to be there for him as much as possible anytime he needed me. It's just easy to get stuck in all the "what ifs."

I remember the first time I saw our best friend Adam Sisouphanh after Miah died. I was telling him that someone asked me how I was holding up? I put up my arm, flexed it, and said, "my hold up muscle is strong. I'm holding up fine!" Then I laughed. This was a true statement and it became frustrating to me that death, even the death of a close friend had become something I was so conditioned to. I expressed frustration to the machine-like response I have to death. Even at the funeral, I cried once, which is the same way I've responded to every funeral. No matter who it was or what age. At this funeral, I did share how much Miah's words of love and acceptance, in-spite of my addiction, meant to me how grateful I was for it, and what effect they had on me getting my life together. Then the service at the grave. Interaction with friends and family at the grave and at his parent's house.

Chapter 14

After that, back to work the same day. Preparations for the biggest fitness event of the year in Utah, FitCon! The event I had been preparing myself for since the day I started selling for 1% Fitness. 4 months in the making! We got things ready Thursday after the funeral. Friday I was early and ready to go! Doors opened, excitement, pitches, people!... I bombed, I closed one person on a meal plan.

One that entire day. I didn't take a break, I didn't stop pitching or working, and I only sold one! We finished that night around 10pm. I went home, spent some time with the girls, and went to bed knowing I had to be up early to be back to the convention at 7:30am. I laid in bed tossing and turning, dissecting my pitch, running through every person I spoke to that day. Identifying mistakes, pitching, pitching, pitching. Imaginary pitches perfecting every word, my mind looping this on instant repeat.

I didn't fall asleep until after 3am at the earliest. This is what my mind does, it obsesses, takes the goal and picks apart anything and everything that stands in the way of that goal. Meaning my mistakes. Then it perfects the path to success. I believe you cannot improve anything without taking 100% responsibility. You will always have an excuse or a cop-out. Successful people take responsibility for everything, even if parts of the situation are outside of their control.

In a case like that, allowing an element to be missed or to rely on someone or something not capable of completing successfully is the mistake. It must be this way because looking at it like this forces the mind to create a successful solution, being sure to calculate and navigate all possible outcomes. Welcome to my mind! When faced with a problem or potential failure, it snaps into action and covers every possibility. My mind creates an end all. Sometimes that end seems like it will never come. My mind just relentlessly loops. That night, the looping didn't end. I only fell asleep when I became so exhausted that nothing could keep me awake.

6am came quick that Saturday morning, I hit the snooze button a couple times. Then got up, got ready, had coffee listened to my motivational hype (YouTube motivations), driving to the event. Then my war song (Last of the Mohicans, bagpipe rendition) after grabbing more coffee and pulling into the parking lot. I was one of the first in the building just before 7:30am. The doors didn't even open until 9am. I hung out getting my mind right. My caffeine choice that morning was a cold brew coffee with 3 shots of espresso, no ice. Co-workers started to show up, set up underway, almost game time!

I forgot to mention, there was a Las Vegas trip incentive on the line. Not that I needed that, but it's always nice to have a reward for something you already know you're going to win! Needless to say, I was not leading the incentive race going into the last day.

Saturday was a different story, from doors open until after doors closed all I did was pitch. Occasional quick bathroom break, drink of caffeine, chug a yogurt drink. No joke, other than seeing a good friend and throwing the kids in the air real-quick. All I did was pitch, pitch, pitch. Close, close, close!

Somewhere around 2pm (5 hours in), I hit a space I had never experienced before. No food, little hydration, pitch after pitch. I went into a 3rd person space, everything was in slow motion, I wondered where I was pulling energy from. I could hear myself speaking and figured it was going to sound awful but as the words came out of my mouth, I heard my tone, my pace, my words, my conviction. God Damn! I had never heard me pitch better!

As I said, it was like I was a 3rd party or a spectator hearing this. Some would call it an out of body experience. Looking back on it, it was definitely spiritual in a way I had never experienced before. At the end of the day when the dust cleared and the smoke settled, I had lost my voice and closed 11 deals that day! Beating my previous best full day by 4. Finishing the convention with 12 sign-ups and yes, winning the Vegas trip.

All accolades aside, it meant so much more than that! It was 4 months of preparation, practice, and improvement. Doubts, fears, and emotional trials pushed through. It was set-backs, and seeming failures pushed through and overcome. It was a win of colossal accomplishment for my process, practice, and skill set! When I got home, I was overwhelmed by everything that had transpired over the previous 2 weeks. I knelt down, kissed the ground, and thanked Miah (I knew he was watching). I thanked my Higher Power, The Universe for working through me in such magnificent ways time and time again!

That was April 22nd, 2017. Our lease at our apartment was up May 16th and that is when we would be moving to Georgia. I worked doubles at the restaurant and 10-14 hours at 1% fitness every day until May 14th, Mother's Day. One of the, if not the busiest day of the year at our restaurant. My last day working for Brio and my best as well. $1,800.00 in sales volume, no breaks, no mistakes! The money I made that day was pretty good too!

Chapter 15

A couple of weeks before moving, I sold one of my cars, so we could have more money for moving to Georgia. And on the second to last day before we left, I sold my other car and we consolidated to one. I suggested packing just as much stuff as we could fit into the Ford Escape and buy new stuff in Georgia. Dom insisted on renting a U-haul and packing as much stuff as possible. We paid to have a complete tow package installed, rented a U-haul, and packed as much as we could fit between the trailer and Escape.

We hit the road heading to Vegas for the 3 night stay I had won for the FitCon sales incentive. We stayed in a nice time share, had a free breakfast, and sales presentation the next morning. They were hard selling time shares and they were pretty good at it. I always appreciate watching a sales presentation, especially when the company has a good system and process in place. At the end, they gave us a choice of a free-gift even though we didn't buy.

I chose the $80.00 gift card, then used it to teach Suraya a valuable life lesson. I told her I was rewarding her for being so well behaved throughout the 2-hour sales presentation and gave her the gift card. I explained I wanted to pay her for her time and did my best to help her understand money comes quickly and easily if we do something to earn it and believe it does.

While driving to Vegas within the first few hours our check engine light came on! I put some fuel treatment in the tank immediately, we got new tires, and an oil change in Vegas and we decided to go for it and hope for the best. We enjoyed the strip, the lights, the Bellagio fountain, and our time share.

I have to take a couple steps back... I'm only talking about the positive of this part of the journey. Like everything is just easy smooth sailing. The fact of the matter is 3 nights before leaving to begin our journey it nearly didn't happen. To even have this move be considered a possibility, Dom and I had been working our asses off! Literally. For example, we celebrated Valentine's day with quick little nice gestures back and forth spread over a few days. Reason being, Valentine's day, we both worked doubles. Her at her restaurant, me at mine Dom got home later than I did, around 11:30pm. We still did sweet things for each other. Surprised each other with bubble baths, candy, notes, candles, it was nice.

Saturday night, May 13th, the night before Mother's Day, again I had worked a double. We were super busy, and I literally ate nothing all day, had no breaks, worked straight through. I knew I needed to eat something. I was past the point of exhaustion. Dom had a surprise for me, she wouldn't tell what other than it was a special night. She wanted me to hurry home because she was preparing a hot bah with candles and a very romantic massage. Well no matter how much I wanted to be in the moment, appreciate what was going on, and soak it all in, every time I tried to relax and enjoy, my mind just went 100% to food. Dom was being caring, loving, and excited to show appreciation. She planned and prepared a romantic sensual evening and I was not able to receive or reciprocate in the least. As erotic as it all was, my mind and body was lifeless unless it was anything to do with food.

This nearly ended our relationship. The next day, Mother's Day morning, Dom was shut down, closed off, and unreceptive to anything. No gifts, no apologies, nothing I tried at all. After everything I tried was rejected, I blew up! My mom used to blow up and completely lose her temper. Scream, yell, slam doors, and maybe hit something. After it was all done, she couldn't recall much, she'd blackout every time.

I wish I had that luxury. When I blow up it's like I have no control over what I'm doing. I'm coherent, see clear. It's like slow motion, I remember every detail. I yell, scream, break and punch things. If that doesn't get my point across or create the effect I want, I get more extreme, slapping, wrestling, choking, head butt or kick things, and or people. Plainly speaking whatever or whoever set me off. That Sunday morning it didn't get past the first stage, Dom left to go to the gym, and I had to be to work for another double.

When I say I was depleted the night before, I mean for 2 or more months at the least. I Was working 14-17 hour-days between the 3 sources of income and preparing for Georgia, doing everything I could do to make sure we had enough money to make the move. We weren't going there with jobs or a place to move into. Hell, we didn't even decide Savannah until a couple weeks before leaving. With pretty much every single action I took the pit in my stomach grew. Especially when selling my cars. I can't even explain how nerve racking it was. I just know the stress and anxiety in my stomach was uncomfortable like nothing I had experienced before!

The night of Mother's Day I drove up to Bountiful, UT I was meeting a guy to sell my other car to. I was so consumed pushing forward with everything I had to get to Georgia that I hadn't looked closely enough to realize Dom had sent me a long text, long long. She called me because she realized I hadn't read it. I took the time to read it while she was on the phone. We had a back and forth and I had one of my blow ups that hit the second degree.

Luckily, I was by myself in the car, so it was punching the steering wheel, screaming, and more punching. I called off selling the car that night. Even though she said something about journeying to Georgia together, then going our separate ways or something I can't quite remember. We had quite a bit of blow ups as we were pushing for the move. Some worse than others, all very draining. We'd somehow find a way to keep going. I get very obsessive when I decide I'm going to do something and I'm stubborn well beyond reason. I will sacrifice EVERYTHING to succeed and that along with my anger, and wandering eye are the reasons Dom and I aren't together anymore.

This is the most difficult part of the book for me to write. It is not in the original publishing. I know it is a very important part of my story to share, with hesitancy I must. Diving past the surface of this issue, I have been a physically abusive partner. I can't even imagine how devastating it is for the abused and I won't try to go into that because it would belittle the serious damage these actions cause. My anger, when it takes control, reminds me of that first chug of the bottle of liquor. The warming of the belly that flows through the body! The rush, the numbing, the slowing of motor skills. The acting with complete abandon. Even waking up in the morning feeling hungover and depleted. When I'm not staying in tune spiritually my vices, mind and body seek the addict comforts.

Being able to recall every action with complete clarity has been a living nightmare. Replaying the videos of my horrendous actions. Knowing with every cell in my being that those actions had a powerful negative affect on the innocent Suraya. My mind denied the severity of my actions for months, it wouldn't even allow me to acknowledge the depth of the damage and the results of my actions until 3 months after the girls had left Georgia. Even at that point, I was only able to look at the surface. My introspection and self-reflection have been a long path, very difficult to face. Recalling my actions and owning up to them scares my soul and rattles my being. I question if I am capable of being in a relationship, scared to get into another, not wanting to risk a repeat. Not wanting to damage me or any other people like that again. It's a crippling hole to crawl out of. I know I've improved in understanding, controlling, and releasing my anger with healthier and better outlets. I know this because Dom and I still spend time together and situations I have blown up over don't affect me the way they used to. I've also watched myself develop over the last year and a half in a high-stress job and witnessed my own reactions to shit hitting the fan in a catastrophic way. Sometimes I want to punch things, but I react much better and don't. But I still have that fear in the back of the mind, the subconscious. What if? What if something triggers me to the depth? How will I react?

The weekend of Feb. 23rd, 2019 I was blessed with one of the greatest experiences I have been gifted. I flew Dom and Suraya in for a late Christmas present Dom and I came together to fulfill a promise we made to Suraya June of 2017 to take her to Disney World! We spent two days there then went to Clearwater, FL. So we could enjoy the beach and the ocean. Driving home that Monday night I was in a euphoric space, floating! I was able to witness my amends followed through to completion. I could see in Dom's demeanor, in her face, body language, and actions in life. That the damage I had caused in our relationship had been healed and that I didn't need to worry about my actions negatively affecting her or Suraya anymore. It was an overwhelming buzz flowing through my being, 1 ½ years in the making that would not have been possible without deep introspection of the ugly truth, commitment to being a man of my word, and taking full responsibility to ensure Suraya and Dom healed from those deep wounds.

Back in Vegas, we had fun. We also had arguments and blow ups, one, the night before taking off to Georgia that mildly hit the second degree... unfortunately, Regardless, Saturday morning we hit the road for Georgia and arrived in Savannah, GA Sunday, May 21st around 4pm! First thing we did was show the girls the beach and the ocean for their first time! Dom said we didn't have time to swim, I told her I knew, and we wouldn't. I just wanted to show them. Of course, we swam! Dom was the one that had to stay longer once it was time to leave. It was beautiful.

We left the beach and drove through a close by neighborhood looking for places to rent. There was one for sale, so we called and left a message about looking to rent, then we checked into a hotel. That evening the owner of the house called and left us a message. Dom spoke to her, explained our situation, and we set up a time to meet her in the morning. We met, liked the house, and agreed to a move in date of May 25th (3 days out). We parked the U-haul at the house and got another hotel for 3 nights.

Finally, move in day! Everything went well, I had been applying for jobs bussing and serving and researching to try to decide what restaurants I wanted to walk into and apply at. So, Friday, the day after moving in, I was able to properly get cleaned up for an interview I lined up. Then head to other restaurants I wanted to apply in person at. My first interview, at The Landings, a golf course restaurant. Went well and they told me they'd be contacting me for a second interview which would be more to make it official than anything. We left there and went straight to The Pirates House! A tourist trap that has been featured on Travel Channel on multiple occasions. Established in 1967 it has quite a name and history. I walked in, asked for an application and a pen, filled it out then and there. I asked if they wanted my resume emailed or if they want a physical copy of it? The hostess went to ask and when she asked the GM decided to interview me right then. We went over everything he asked about my experience. I told him about my best day at Brio, Mother's Day. He told me, "I'm sold, you sold me." Hired on the spot! Starting just a few days later. Place to move, job to start within the first 5 days!... Off to the beach!

Everything was going amazing. The girls were experiencing new things. Like the beach and cockroaches! Adjusting well to humidity and bugs. A couple times they mentioned other bugs, I just figured it was cockroaches, maybe June bugs. We decided to go swimming in the ocean that Saturday night. It was amazing. Tybee beach, sky full of stars, warm Atlantic water!

As we were swimming, we noticed the ocean would light up faintly. As we looked closer, sometimes it would light up more than others, and we were loving watching the ocean light up under our fingertips! Once in the car we googled it and found that it was bioluminescent algae! It was amazing and beautiful! Such a great experience for all of us!

That night I was lying in bed and felt something on my leg, I turned my phone light on and found a little bug. Figured it was just a cockroach and set it on the rug. As I laid back down something was different about it. My mind thought, bedbug! I googled it and sure as shit, it was a bedbug! I sat up in bed with an anxiety I can't put words to. It was strong enough that it woke Dom out of her sleep. We weren't able to sleep. We checked the house. Found dead bedbugs in one of the couches left behind. A couple more on the underside of our bed and about 10 on the edge and underside of Suraya's bed. We had all been bitten in the couple nights there. Suraya got it the worst by far, which still breaks my heart to this day.

We discussed a few different options and decided to get our deposit back and find a different place. No U-haul and the risk of bed bugs. We left 70-80% of our belongings when we left that house. Suraya's biggest favorite toys, our beds, books, dressers, pretty much anything we couldn't wash and fit in the Escape. After the fact we realized we left Suraya's baby picture scrap book and a couple very important journals. Still a frustration to this day.

We went to the laundry mat and spent 8 hours and $120.00 washing and drying everything to make sure we rid it of any bedbugs or eggs. As it got late (early in the morning), Suraya tired out and needed to lay down. Luckily right then the blankets and pillows finished drying. I took a blanket and folded it up with another for her to lay on. Then took a big blanket and tied a corner to the hanger post on a folding table to make a tent for her. She loved it and was super excited to sleep in her tent! I then went into the bathroom, broke down, and cried. We had no place to make our home, hotels would drain our money and I failed my family in a disastrous way!

We left for our journey May 17th with $4,000.00 dollars total! We got to Savannah May 21st stayed in hotels 4 nights, that house 3 nights, got most of our money back from the landlord, but then stayed in hotels until the night of June 5th. 12 nights in hotels.

Oh yeah, we also had this little mis-hap in searching for another place. I was communicating with a man who called himself "Michael Scott." "In the military, man of god and very faithful." Texas phone number, "stationed in Maryland" owner of this house in Pooler, GA about 25 minutes away from Savannah. We went to the house, walked through it. Some things added up, most things didn't.

Examples; he said there was a washer and dryer and dryer. There wasn't. I asked him if the house had been sprayed for bugs because there were dead ones clearly indicating the house hadn't been sprayed. He said, "no, no need to spray, no bugs," which in hind sight is a statement no homeowner in the south would ever make. It raised a red flag but was quickly forgotten in the scramble to get my family into a house. He told us to Moneygram $1,000.00 and we would get the code to the lock box on the door with the key to the house in it. Every red flag in my body went off! He kept repeating his pitch, I'm a man of faith, a good Christian man of god, with a family of my own. If you feel better sending $500.00 first, then the rest after that's fine. Before you do any of that you'll need to sign the lease agreement and move in agreement or at least send them over soon after sending the money. Because I do have another family that is going to move in if you don't. I was more than skeptical we were getting scammed. Dom and I decided to have this man send a picture of his license. He called, spoke to me shortly, then Dom. We sent the money "on faith." Vulnerability is a hell of an emotion to exploit. It will outweigh all logic and common sense!

The next day I started my job and confirmed what we had figured. We got scammed out of $500.00, still no place to move into, and our finances draining, stressed is an understatement. I worked as much as possible, but training limited my hours. Outside of work hours, we did everything we could to find a place to move into.

Chapter 16

I noticed that if I allowed my stress and fear to dictate how I acted around the girls, their energy would shift and follow. I realized anytime I was with them, it was important to stay composed. No matter what! The girls would mirror whatever emotions were exhibited, so I had to be mindful. Dom was calling and visiting anything and everything we could find for rent. That's all she did while I was working. Once I was off, we'd do as much as possible to visit or find more places. It was difficult because most offices were closed when I got off. Still, we would drive around and ask people as they left church if they knew of anything or anybody renting. We got some leads from that and Dom was able to follow up with everything.

I remember one night in our hotel I could feel Dom's anxiety. It woke me up out of my sleep. I went over to her and held her. She expressed, "we don't have the money to move into any of these places, why am I even searching?" It broke my heart to hear such a powerful fear for the first time. The second I heard it, I could feel how heavy it was and it hurt to know she'd not expressed it to me before. I assured her that I would be able to source the money, that she just needed to find us a place and I'd make sure we got into it. I promised her it'd be fine and told her I wish she would've spoken about this instead of holding it in and worrying herself sick.

My dad loaned us $4,000.00 between 2 payments, and with 1% Fitness employment verification (even though I didn't technically work there) we got approved to move into a 2 bed 2.5 bath town home June 6th, 2017. After work, I stayed up until 3am to organize, hang and put up clothes. We had pillows and blankets. Ne beds, no couches, or chairs. We had my laptop that we used to watch movies on, and each other!

The next day, June 7th, was Suraya's birthday, so I wanted the house straightened up for her. We got her a dress, a princess crown, and a birthday girl banner. The girls enjoyed downtown while I worked. Then we all enjoyed it together for a bit once I got off. We finished the evening at Chuck E. Cheese's and then a movie at home! It was a great birthday. 3 days later was Dom's birthday! We enjoyed River St. downtown, went out to dinner, and just had quality family time. Still to this day Dom says it was one of her favorite birthday's ever!

We began our journey with Suraya's cat and hamster. Unfortunately, the hamster died before we made it into our new place. Raya wanted to give a proper burial, so we went to the beach and said our official goodbyes. Kitty was my best friend... well 3rd after Suraya and Dom. Kitty and I used to chase each other around the house and play tag. When I would call him and pat on my chest, he'd run in and lay down right on my chest like a dog.

One night he ran in and laid that way. He was scratching his head on my chin more than usual. I turned on the phone light and discovered he had fleas. We steamed the house, stormed the laundry mat again. Got some flea shampoo for him, but after the ordeal with the bedbugs and seeing how many fleas he had on him, we just couldn't risk it. We abandoned kitty by tossing him down by the marsh. We felt we had no better choice. It was heart breaking and still hurts my heart deeply anytime I think about it. In hind sight, I wonder often if I made the wrong decision. We just felt it was too big of a risk. The bedbug trauma had us reeling. We all cried that night then went on with rebuilding our lives.

I was working as much as possible. We were living on the minimum we could. Ramen noodles, tv dinners. We would go out to eat to try to do something enjoyable, watch movies, and eat ice cream or popcorn! We also went to the LDS church and asked for help. The bishop said they would pay the rent for us for two months to help free up some money so we could get some bedding and other comforts. We went to church a couple times. Suraya seemed to enjoy it and it really was helpful to us in multiple ways. I'm very grateful for the help the LDS church has given me throughout my life. I can honestly say I would not be the man I am today without the huge influence it has had on my entire life. Taking on many different shapes and forms of help in growth and advancement. With financial help in my life as well as philosophical. I am eternally grateful the LDS organization.

I was working as much as possible and we were able to get a futon, some decorations, and kitchen ware for the place. We went to the beach and tried to do as many things as possible to enjoy ourselves and our time together.

Dom and I would still have fights here and there. Some bad and some mild. I stayed in a hotel a couple times just to sleep and not do anything stupid. There were still explosions that went too far, and I got physical. Dom and I were growing further and further apart. I didn't know what to do. I'd say a strong love language for both of us is "quality time." Neither of us were getting that. I tried my best to show my love by providing, supporting, taking care of, handling any and all responsibilities to help the family. So that's what I did no matter what.

After one fight Dom asked what I was going to change? I told her nothing because I don't believe I'm doing anything wrong, I'm going to keep taking care of business like I have been. Then I went and did some late-night laundry, so we'd all have clean clothes, then I tidied up, so we'd have a clean house. Then I went to bed so I could get up and go to work so we'd have money to do some of the things we wanted to do.

Raya loved going to the laundry mat anytime, every time! She'd get so excited it blew my mind! It amazed me to think how important it is for us to keep the mind of a child as we age. My adult mind remembers the horrific time in the laundry mat, breaking into tears in the bathroom, the overwhelming reality of us being homeless and walking away from so many things. Important documents, journals, photo albums! Scared that every-single thing was completely infested. She remembers the adventure of the imagination and staying in the awesome tent that Mark made. Sleeping on a cool bed, getting to stay up late and help her mom and me! Oh, how beautiful and amazing the child's mind is! Such a blessing and so grounding, so effective at calming the adult stresses if you allow it to. That little girl continues to bless my mind and my life, through remembering the past as well as interacting with her still today.

Part of the agreement with Suraya's biological father and us moving to Georgia was that she'd fly home for a week over the 4th of July. Her mom went with her. We were still strapped for cash, so I had to ask my dad to help us buy one of the plane tickets. We couldn't afford the $660.00. While they were out of town, I scheduled myself to work doubles everyday they were gone. 8 doubles in a row! It was exhilarating, watching my momentum grow. Seeing my serving skills improve so quickly. Earning money, handling rushes of guests. It was near the end of this 8 days I realized I was better at serving than I ever cared to be. Not that I was great or anything like that, I was just better than I ever wanted to be at serving. This was a good realization, it was the beginning of my mind searching for a sales job again. I wasn't sure where or what, just really wanted back into sales.

After a couple weeks my mind decided brokering yachts was the answer. I took Raya and we drove to yacht yards and boat dealerships to find out as much as I could about becoming a yacht broker. I didn't walk the yacht/boat walk, but I still tried anything I could think of. Called in friends and connections for help, researched as much as possible. Emailed big names in the industry. The ones selling super yachts! Even applied for labor jobs at Thunderbolt Marina just to be around yachts and learn from the ground up. I obsessed about that for a month or so.

Dom and Suraya got back, and I had 3 days in a row off for us to enjoy. We went on night swims and beach walks on Hilton Head and Tybee. We enjoyed good restaurants and sleep in days, it was great! Then back to work. I worked 50-60 hours a week and things were falling into place. The second to last week of

July, I bought a pedal bike from a co-worker for $50.00 It was a purple girl's bike that rode a little funny, but it got the job done.

Dom was going to the gym twice a day keeping up with her regimen, pushing for her goal of winning an Olympic gold medal! Something she seriously can do and has been aiming for since Jr. High! Suraya and I got to hang out and spend quality time! Sometimes we'd just sleep in, other days we'd create adventures, do arts and crafts, or go explore! We have been close since day one, but we grew closer during our time in Georgia. Breakfast and dancing, crafts and wrestling, fighting, or "karate" as Suraya says it! We'd play all day and night if we could!

One night I'll never forget, Suraya was asking her mom about Dom and me, my role, our family, and us. When she was done, she looked at me, got super excited, jumped up and yelled DAD! Something I'm still very proud of to this day! Even after all the arguing, fighting, and all the shit, I know, to this day the love that little girl and I share is very real!

It breaks my heart to recall this because just a few days later Dom packed the car to head back to Utah for good. Our fighting was more frequent and very escalated! The cops were called on one occasion, the townhome neighbor could hear our shouting and screaming. She could hear it escalate to physical abuse, we both sustained damages. As the cops were questioning me, my uber to work showed up, and they let me leave.

A couple days later a female co-worker made an inappropriate joke, I laughed and didn't do anything else. That was the last straw for Dom. Thursday, August 3rd, for the last time, the girls dropped me off at work and hit the road to head to Utah. I remember saying goodbye in the parking lot on that hot sunny day. When I look back on that day (and I have quite often), I find it strange. I wasn't scared, nervous, or upset. There was no fear or anxiety as I said goodbye, I knew I'd be fine. There was a calmness within like I had never experienced before. It was time to go to war!

Top picture is the one I took personally, bottom is from my vision board

We were saving money in the jar to take Suraya to Disney World. I think it was about $760.00 I gave it plus a little more to Dom to

get back to Utah. I don't remember what was in my bank account, but I knew I'd be fine. My job had proven it could produce as-long as I showed up. And my life just simplified.

Section 3: Win

Chapter 17

My bike ride was 8.3 miles one way, a total of 16.6 miles round trip to and from work. It took 45-50 min to get there and I never cared how long it took to get back home. After working 6-12 hours on my feet I was rarely in any hurry to get home. I always had a respect and admiration for those that walked, rode a bike, or took the bus, to accomplish what they needed to. When I received the gift of this experience, I embraced it! I Ubered a couple times but it was too expensive just to be lazy.

The laundry mat was the most difficult part. Fill the backpack, wash and dry and killing time (audio books, Science of Getting Rich, As A Man Thinketh). It was the worst when I'd put it off until I had to do it before working a double. Those days were exhausting, and I could feel myself dragging.

I remember there was a heatwave for a few days. I would hear my guests at the restaurant complaining about how hot it was.

All I could think about was the 8.3 miles I just biked in. The heat never crossed my mind, I had to be to work. I made sure my mindset stayed in the space if WIT (Whatever It Takes). In that space there was no option, I had no choice. I had the opportunity to succeed on my own in Georgia! A goal of mine for almost 4 years. There was no other plan. This was it, it didn't matter what happened, I was going to power through and succeed. And I did!

Before the girls left, I had already arranged to fly to Jackson, MS to hang out with Curt and Mitch Ford, knock some doors, sell some alarms, and hang out with some of the old crew. Like I mentioned before, my mind wanted to get back to sales and it was doing WIT to make it happen! I flew into Jackson, but the boys were 2 ½ hours north in Tupelo.

At the time, my license had been expired for nearly 3 years, so I had to Uber. It was a $280.00 Uber ride. I met up with Mitch just before 5:30pm and got right to work! It had been about 5 years since I had knocked doors, but I love that shit! So, it was easy to get back in the swing of things! In my opinion, there's nothing like it! The nerves that kick in when you knock on that first door of the day. The questions circling your head, can I sell this person? Are they sane or completely insane? Are they nice? Rude? Ugly? Pretty? That first pitch, is it going to be smooth, choppy, good, or awful? Then the door opens... it's go time!

All the noise in your head silences. You snap into action! Your tone, body language, eye contact, revert to what's been trained and practiced thousands of times! Whether you sell the first door or not, you get a stranger to open-up and speak to you about their neighborhood, the neighbors, and what kind of problems they know of in the area.

If you sell the first house it's real nice! Then you have the rest of the day to take that momentum and sell a couple more! Selling the last house of the night may be the best feeling ever! You just got told, "no" for 6-7 hours and with your last opportunity, you closed! As far as I'm concerned, there's not too many things better! Drop me off in a new neighborhood where I don't know anybody or anything and by the end of the day, I've earned anywhere from $500-$2,500.00! One of the greatest feelings in the world! Producing from nothing, just words, a product or service, and WIT!

I sold two accounts my 2nd day which was a Thursday. The next day, I had someone call the cops. After speaking to the cop, while wearing Mitch Ford's name badge (since I wasn't licensed or registered to knock doors) and I didn't even have a valid driver's license. I was scared shitless, I acted stupid and confused, told him I was headed right to the city hall to get it taken care of.

He let me go, then asked for some info on our company. I gave him one of our welcome packets that we give new customers and he drove away. I couldn't believe I got out of it!... My acting worked! It did get in my head though, I didn't sell another account. I earned $1,000.00 which I considered a failure but still earned some money even after all my expenses, so it was okay. More importantly I was able to spend some time with the boys and get some sales practice in!

When I returned to the restaurant, business was a little slower than I was used to. Still making money and doing fine but it wasn't busy season anymore. Same routine, riding the bike to and from work and to do the laundry. I listened to the audiobook Science Of Getting Rich by Wallace D. Wattles. I would speed it up on audible and it would finish right before I'd get home every night. My round trip to and from work was the perfect amount of time to finish it. I listened to it every day I worked. I listened to it on repeat, this routine started sometime soon after Dom and Suraya left. It's a metaphysical thinking book, talks about how becoming rich is the most important skill for us to possess, that to develop in mind, soul, and body. We must have the free use of things. Society is so organized that we must have plenty of money in order to become the possessor of things, therefore the basis of all advancement for man must be the science of getting rich. That God wants us to become rich so we can enjoy fine things and develop the talents and gifts that God has given us. That he wants us to enjoy these things because it is God himself that enjoys them through us. It repeats that we must stay in the creative mind state and entirely rise above the competitive mindset.

"chapter 17

Summary of The Science of Getting Rich

There is a thinking stuff from which all things are made, and which, in its original state, permeates, penetrates, and fills the interspaces of the universe.

A thought in this substance produces the thing that is imaged by the thought.

Man can form things in his thought, and by impressing his thought upon formless substance can cause the thing he thinks about to be created.

In order to do this, man must pass from the competitive to the creative mind; otherwise he cannot be in harmony with the Formless Intelligence, which is always creative and never competitive in spirit.

Man may come into full harmony with the Formless Substance by entertaining a lively and sincere gratitude for the blessings it bestows upon him. Gratitude unifies the mind of man with the intelligence of Substance, so that man's thoughts are received by the Formless. Man can remain upon the creative plane only by uniting himself with the

Formless Intelligence through a deep and continuous feeling of gratitude .

Man must form a clear and definite mental image of the things he wishes to have, to do, or to become; and he must hold this mental image in his thoughts, while being deeply grateful to the Supreme that all his desires are granted to him. The man who wishes to get rich must spend his leisure hours in contemplating his Vision, and in earnest thanksgiving that the reality is being given to him. Too much stress cannot be laid on the importance of frequent contemplation of the mental image, coupled with unwavering faith and devout gratitude. This is the process by which the impression is given to the Formless, and the creative forces set in motion."

The creative energy works through the established channels of natural growth, and of the industrial and social order. All that is included in his mental image will surely be brought to the man who follows the instructions given above, and whose faith does not waver. What he wants will come to him through the ways of established trade and commerce.

In order to receive his own when it shall come to him, man must be active; and this activity can only consist in more than filling his present place. He must keep in mind the Purpose to get rich through the realization of his mental image. And he must do, every day, all that can be done that day, taking care to do each act in a successful manner. He must give to every man a use value in excess of the cash value he receives, so that each transaction makes for more life; and he must so hold the Advancing Thought that the impression of increase will be communicated to all with whom he comes in contact.

The men and women who practice the foregoing instructions will certainly get rich; and the riches they receive will be in exact proportion to the definiteness of their vision, the fixity of their purpose, the steadiness of their faith, and the depth of their gratitude."

This book and the philosophies in it are deduced from works written by Hagel and Emerson. Emerson's Compensation essay, the one that that I mentioned earlier in this book, is part of the inspiration for The Science of Getting Rich! It wasn't until writing this book that the power of this evolution in my own life's experience had the time to sink in, and its full depth hit me like a ton of bricks! It makes my entire body tingle to look back and see the path line up so clearly, to see the power of intelligent substance has been guiding my growth simply because of knowledge, belief, and action! That this theory was put to the test and the result could not have been anything different, to see the full truth in its glorious purity!... It's emotionally moving and gives me understanding when I look back at all the times I've broken down and cried due to the gratitude that overwhelms my being, how could I not cry?

Chapter 18

The first week of September 2017, hurricane Irma was circling East of Savannah. I had never been in a hurricane warning area before. I listened to the news and everybody's 2 cents. I didn't know what to make of it. All I knew was the restaurant was probably going to close and finances were already tighter than I wanted.

As the days went on, I remember texting Dom. She asked about the hurricane and I told her they say it's going to be bad... I remember this clearly because my heart fluttered, and a tear dropped from each eye. It shocked me.

I was trying to line up something to be able to leave town and work somehow. I texted about 15 people, nothing. Then my friend Brett Triana texted and said he'd be in Minnesota for two weeks selling TV packages. That was Wednesday night. Thursday, I helped my buddy and co-worker Darren board up his windows for the storm. By 3pm that

144

day I called the restaurant to tell them I was flying to Minnesota for two weeks and would return.

I had my dad help me book a flight from ATL to Minnesota (MSP), while I booked a flight from Savannah to Atlanta. I did it that way because it was much cheaper. Money was tight. I had changed the money jar's purpose to "the license and car jar." I was saving up to pay off the $1,000.00 fine that had my license suspended in Boston. It had been 2 ½ years that I drove around on an expired license because I didn't want to pay that fine. I felt wronged by Boston Municipal.

That my lawyer got me off any financial obligations they said I had to pay. Of course, all that mentally did was hurt me. Without a car, I could no longer run from it. I also had a speeding ticket in Georgia and driving on an expired license I had to appear in court for. This happened before the girls left when I was arguing with Dom while driving. Anyway, I had

$630.00 in the jar and a couple hundred in my account after buying my flight. It was time to go ALL IN!

I took all the money from the jar and packed for my flight. I asked 4 different people for a ride to the airport before I found one. The mayhem of the airport before a hurricane! My first flight got cancelled because they were flying the airline employees out. It auto rescheduled a flight that would've landed after my flight to Minnesota. I manually rescheduled for a late flight Friday night.

My ride picked me up about 30 minutes later than planned but still plenty of time. I walked in and it was empty. No TSA, only a few employees. All the workers were confused how I had a boarding pass. Exit security called in and a couple people came through. The plane was there but they couldn't let me through because TSA was closed. That flight was a return flight to ATL that rarely flies with passengers. If I got there a little earlier before TSA closed, I would have been on that plane.

Delta didn't have anything available first thing in the morning. As the lady checked flights it just so happened one passenger cancelled their flight, so the lady was able to get me on it! She took me downstairs to the customer service office to get me some snacks and coffee. We were just chatting and as I told her I didn't have a vehicle and was just going to hang out in the airport. She, without saying anything, started to call hotels. I told her she didn't have to, but she insisted and said Delta would take care of it. She found a room, printed my voucher, and lined up the shuttle.

I was so grateful! I didn't know how to express it. I got to the hotel starving, but the restaurant was closed. I walked over the freeway overpass to the restaurant area. The only place open was Arby's and only the drive-through was open. They wouldn't let me order without a car. I asked a guy to put in an order. He seemed sketched out and said no, I asked another guy and he said yes. By the time I got back and ate it was almost 1am. I had the shuttle scheduled at 5 am, and I was so tired I was scared if I went to sleep, I wouldn't wake up for the shuttle. So I didn't sleep. Add to that, the entire week leading up to this I got little to no sleep because my anxiety from financial and hurricane stress was so high. I couldn't shut down my mind to save my life!

Boarding went fine, I slept on the plane and then when we landed, I found a spot on the ground in the terminal waiting area it. It was Saturday morning and my next flight wasn't until Sunday afternoon. I laid down on the ground and passed out!

I woke up pissed off! Because of the damn Mexican music, they were blasting through the speakers! Turns out I was next to the fucking Puerto Rico terminal, so they were blasting that shit!

I was disoriented, my body was in pain, and I was severely under-rested. I went to Buffalo Wild Wings 2 or 3 times that day, to eat and watch sports. I wandered around ATL's gigantic airport in wonder, went on an adventure with some random girl that I started talking to at B-Dubs. She tried to get me on her flight, but it didn't work.

Then back to night in the airport and everything shut down. I was trying to find somewhere to sleep, laid down on the floor a couple times but my body wasn't having it. As I was wandering, I found a Delta blanket and pillow. Have no idea who's they were, but I waited a while, then took them, went up to a lounge area pushed some chairs together and went to sleep. It was okay sleep all things considered. Looking back on it, I would have been much better off getting a hotel near ATL airport, but I was trying to save money. A few hours later I was on my flight, slept, then caught a shuttle to a hotel near Mall of America.

I checked into my room then shortly after Brett and his boss Alex started texting me. Alex said he would come pick me up. By that time, I had checked into my room, eaten a good meal at Outback Steakhouse and was in bed about to pass out. It was 5 or 6pm. I looked at the phone and knew I was about to be at a shared lake house with 14 other sales guys. I was so exhausted and had so little sleep, I knew I needed to get one good night's rest in while I could before jumping into the fire! I slept for 14 hours!

Chapter 19

While I was eating the night before, I booked my greyhound to a pickup spot near the lake house. It was a 3-hour bus ride that didn't leave until 5:30 pm. I spent the free time I had taking in the Mecca that is Mall of America, Minnesota. They had lockers, so I was able to store my bag (a luxury, after toting that thing around ATL for 27 hours). I got my haircut (with some beard work done) and cleaned up. I wandered and checked out shops, restaurants, amusement parks, displays, art features. This mall has everything, it varies from 3-4 stories high, movie theatres, all the top retail names, arcades, games, roller coasters. Zip lines, mini golf, ice skating rink, the biggest Lego display you'll ever see! If you want to expand your mind and experience something that will force you to think BIGGER, this is it! It took me 3 days to wrap my mind around what I just took in!

After much-needed sleep and some alone time to explore, I was ready to get after it! I had been studying the sales script and outline repeatedly throughout my traveling. Anytime I could sit and read that's what I was studying. I got picked up at the bus stop by my boy Brett and we went to the lake house where I met the rest of the crew. It was a full house with a beautiful lake view in the back yard. Fire pit, game rooms, pool table, ping pong. The house was supplied well with food and everyone was doing what they could to get this sales job down. Most of them were new to knocking doors. The only thing that was new to me was selling DirecTv, but I was confident in my knocking and sales ability.

I sold my first day out and closed 4 the first week, only had 3 install though. After seeing a differently managed door knocking office, I continued going all in! I called the restaurant on Sunday after that first week and told them I wouldn't be coming back. That next time I was in town I would bring a formal letter but wanted to let them know sooner than later I was quitting. The next week I sold 0 the first 3 days. The regional manager, Alex had me knock with him that Thursday. He sold two and put one in my name, said he doesn't expect reps to knock with him for free. The next day I sold 3 on my own!

During the two weeks in MN everybody had a good time, we played team games of mafia, fished, kayaked, bonfires, it was great! We enjoyed beautiful sunsets and lightning storms over the lake, it was just a wonderful environment.

One of the guys out there, Tanner Lyman was planning on doing a working traveling journey eventually making it to the next blitz in Colorado the 2nd and 3rd week of October. I had just quit my job and had no return flight to Savannah. Tanner and I put together a vague working and traveling route. The only thing I had to do was be in Savannah Oct. 4th for court. We hit the road, stopped quick in Indiana to sell a few accounts, then hit the road again to find a place to stay. We followed this pattern, stopping to enjoy a Sunday in Chicago, and a day in Knoxville, TN. Other than that it was drive, knock, sell. I was still paying my lease on the townhome in Savannah, so we made it there somewhat quickly to limit hotel stays and save some money. We stayed in Savannah for 1 ½ weeks and left the day after my court date, I just pushed it back to Nov. 29th.

I kept studying the sales script. I was selling enough to pay the bills and travel across the country but just barely. There were some issues with pay being incorrect which was very stressful but got sorted out easily after some frustrating communication.

Tanner is a flat-earth society guy and conspiracy theorist so he's very studied and passionate about his stances. I kept my mouth shut regarding anything that would rile him up because I needed my energy to work and endure.

I am a very particular person. I don't like noise, light, and unnecessary anything. I especially can't stand snoring. Sharing a 6-bunk bedroom with 5 other guys, of course there is snoring. At the cabin, my sleep quality wasn't the best but a couple nights at the end I was able to get into one of the single bedrooms and have true peace and quiet.

I can't sleep with snoring and Tanner snores! I'd put my headphones in and play music at max volume but could still hear his snoring! When it's that loud the only time I fall asleep is after hours of frustration exhausting me enough that I pass out. There were some nights at my place in Savannah I could hear Tanner's snoring through all the walls. All that being said, we enjoyed great times, good restaurants, good conversation and amazing experiences driving and working our way across the country!

I only state these things because I am a highly introverted personality that works in sales and have had to learn how to conserve my energy to survive in conditions that are incredibly outside my comfort zone. Which is a quiet house with the blinds closed, nobody, and nothing making noise.

At the end of our time in Savannah, the Vegas shooting happened. Tanner was consumed by every bit of media coverage that could be found. It was something I've never witnessed on this level before. We spoke of how it didn't add up and seemed to be a complete setup organized by the government. I agree but I don't let shit like that consume me. I watched the spiral and within a couple days, Tanner's mentality turned and was just grim and down. Disturbed and disgusted by the events that grip our world seemingly constructed and carried out by the government or powers that be. He hit that point of, "nothing we do even matters." I did my best to shift it and bring it back, but the energy was too powerful.

We hit the road headed for Arkansas, Tanner has family there, his sister had just had a baby, and we stayed with the family a couple nights. Then hit the road again, another hotel. Neither of us sold the rest of our time heading to Colorado.

Chapter 20

I already planned to make it to Utah after Colorado since I'd be so close. Since I had gone a week without selling, I started putting a business plan together. I ran my numbers and data from my time with 1% Fitness and calculated what kind of production I could contribute being a full time, outside, traveling salesman for them. I reversed engineered the goal of $120,000.00 in one year. A calculation taught in Jordan Belfort's Straightline Persuasion sales training. I listed any and all expos and conventions near them that were good for their industry. After doing the calculation I had to reduce my goal to $73,000.00. After putting together a solid plan, I showed it to Dom. She said, "that looks good, but I think you should talk to Chris."

Chris Woods was talking to Dom back when we were first engaged. I went over, kissed her, and introduced myself. We've been friends ever since. He tried to convince me to work for him brokering logging and sawmilling equipment for 2 years! I knew Dom was right and I knew what my plan was. This plan put my original goal of $120,000.00 in one year back in play!

With my new motivation and help from Bret, I sold 19 accounts during that two weeks in Colorado with 14 coming the last 8 days of the trip. That last week I was on fire! And only one of those 14 was with any help from Brett. The shift came from my mentality.

Chris always told me I needed 3 months of finances saved so that I could learn the job, build up the pipeline, and start making money. I never had 3 months saved up before and didn't have it then. My mind was doing what it was used to, thinking of who I could get to loan me a few thousand dollars. "Who can I get to invest in me and my future?" I knew the people I was going to pitch, I knew how I was going to succeed at it, knew who'd say yes.

While out in Colorado, one of the managers, Kaden Hensley, was having us watch Jordan Belfort's Straightline Persuasion sales seminar lessons. This helped me in numerous ways. Most important was, it reminded me to treat every single person I talked to about my product, as a potential investor! My mind said, "stop putting energy into thinking about who you're going to pitch on lending you money. Put all that energy into every pitch, on every doorstep. Because they are all potential investors!" Once this shift in my mentality occurred, I was selling 2 accounts almost every day!

I got to Utah the night of Oct. 23rd stayed at my parents, caught the front runner up to Salt Lake City, then paid $35.00 to get an Uber up the canyon to Chris's cabin overlooking Solitude Ski Resort. Beautiful cabin with even more beautiful views of the mountains! We spoke about the job, I showed him the plan I had put together and explained how it had led me to him, told him what I had been up to. He challenged my commitment, then asked where I was staying. I told him my parents, and his response was, "nope you're staying here, go get your stuff." I made it back up that night, they had an empty loft at the top of the cabin, it was dope! It was completely open though. 3 boys, Chris's girlfriend and myself. I was finally able to sleep without directly sharing a room with someone. Didn't have to listen to a tv or snoring all night! Still more noise and people than I like, but 1000x better than what the previous 6 ½ weeks was!

We spent the 25th and 26th setting up systems and learning the quick pitch opener, "This is Mark with Lumbermens, calling to see if you have any equipment for sale? Or if you're looking for anything in particular?"

That's about it for formal training. The 27th was game time! I thought I had 2 months of finances covered. I realized quickly I only had 1 month. The first week I went to the gym with Chris but after getting a feel for the job and finances, I understood that I had to take Chris's 3-month learning curve and compress it into 3 weeks! I was scared shitless, I had to constantly battle my mind seeking comfort. It wanted to me to pitch someone on lending me money and investing in me and my future.

I had to continually tell it, we aren't going to do that, put that energy into finding customers to invest! I worked my ass off, I was noting everything with pen and paper because I believe we learn faster that way. I didn't know shit about logging or sawmilling, equipment or anything. I would wake up early and call from about 7am until 5:30pm MST. If I got any pictures of equipment in, I would take care of listing it on Craig's List and Facebook, then I would prioritize my call lists and contacts. Finally, I would google search any of the equipment that got spoken about in my calls.

I had people call in on listings and I would talk to them about the equipment but would never hear back from them. I knew immediately it was because I sounded like an idiot and didn't know what I was talking about. This was costing me money and I wasn't happy about it! I knew I needed to know my equipment better if I was going to have a chance at selling anything.

Austin Woods helped me a lot with equipment and terms for the industry but the best way to learn was talk to the loggers and sawyers about it. I was working as much as I possibly could, to the point that I hit a headspace where I sat and stared at the same part of the mountains for 3 hours straight! I was questioning everything I was doing, the journey that had brought me there, and my dwindling bank account.

I had a buyer Denny Bryant. We established trust and he liked me. I had the machine he wanted and even though my seller was hunting and beyond difficult to deal with or get a hold of, I was able to get just enough info to get Denny and his wife to go through financing. They got approved, I figured out trucking, and while this was going on, Denny gave me a couple pieces of equipment to list for sale. One was a mobile dimensions sawmill. On a Thursday night I got a call from Billy Dykes, he wanted to buy it. Chris helped me close the deal so I could hear what to say, how to say it, and what to do to finalize.

That same night I had my mom cash app me $5.00. I had bills hitting the next morning and I didn't have enough to cover them. Friday Nov. 17th, after those bills hit, I had 13 cents in my bank account. I was sitting at the table with Chris talking to him about it all and we were just laughing.

That same day, money came in for the sawmill, and the tree cutter Denny was buying came in. $25,000.00 for the mill, of which

$4,150.00 was our commission 50/50 split. $72,500.00 also came in of which $10,000.00 was supposed to be our commission 50/50 split! The entire week leading up to this I could not breathe! This was the first time I had large commissions to either gain or lose on the line! My anxiety crippled me, I'd do my best to work through it. Some moments I could, other moments I couldn't.

I say supposed to split $10,000.00 because once we had the money in, my seller changed his price from $60k to $65k cutting the potential commission in half. Then as the communication progressed, my seller pulled the machine entirely and would not let me sell it! He said I questioned his integrity and more so was too impatient and too aggressive. Since he was so difficult to get a hold of and such a large commission was on the line.

I was doing anything I could to get this deal done, I contacted my sellers-family members, sent messages, left countless voicemails. Anything I could do to try to finalize it. He told me he was going to teach me some patience by pulling out on the deal. The entire week leading up to this I couldn't breathe but now this! Holy shit! We did everything we could to pull something off that day.

Then, that night Chris called Sam Wall, his longest working employee. He also brought Austin over, and said, we've got $72,000.00 in the account for this machine lets go find one! Denny had gotten worried to the point that he was already threatening a lawyer. Chris then started to tell me where I fucked up. I was furious at the situation and Chris's sales lesson. I lit up! My face went red as a stop sign, I had to breathe, tell myself to calm down, listen, and hear the lesson. The team found a few machines, Sam took over the customer which pissed me off, but he found the right machine and sold Denny on it. We had the machine loaded and on its way Monday afternoon, we pulled it off! Monday, Nov. 20th I got paid $5,400.00 for two deals! I did it, I found my investors!

Chapter 21

My last week in Utah I went down to the valley and stayed at Jai's. I slept and watched movies a lot! Went to Jared O'brien's grandma's funeral. Jared's like a brother to me and I was glad I could be there to show support and I did know his grandma pretty well too. I visited friends and family, was able to play a good violent turkey bowl that Thanksgiving. Caught up with old friends and prepared to go back to Savannah.

Once I got back to Savannah it was a whole new ball game! Now I had to find motivation in and of myself, for myself by myself. My bike was still my transportation. I bought a washer and dryer to eliminate the laundry mat! Started waking up at 6am, biking to the gym and back, and working my ass off, I had no choice! I make it sound easy, but it was not. I was listening to The Science of Getting Rich almost every day, clarifying my vision, biking, lifting, and trying to eat better.

When I left Utah, I was fatter than I had been in a long time. Hadn't been going to the gym and wasn't eating the best. Sacrifices needed to be made to improve my life.

This new chapter was like making it from Amateur to Professional! The pros required another level of structure and discipline. I had to figure it out and lock it in. I had nobody watching over me, nobody constantly telling me what to do, no schedule I had to follow or answer to. What separates a 15-year career champion, from the 3 to 4-year average pro? Sacrifice, discipline, structure, details, the process! Love for what you do, unwavering desire for greatness, and eternal gratitude for every experience! I had to lock it in, or I would fail. The fear of losing everything, again, fueled me!

My aim was to get my license back. I had to pay for and take an 8-hour class, pay some fees, and pay the $1,000.00 to reinstate. All told it was just shy of $1,400.00. My

December routine was, the gym, a lot of work, and a lot of movies. I also completed Open, by Andre Agassi, a great book! Quite the rollercoaster, amazing to read about how much he truly hates the game of Tennis and was still able to have such an impact on the sport and win as much as he did. I was making between 120-170 calls a day which produced 3 deals in Dec. earning me $6,400.00. I paid the fine, took the class, passed the driving test, and got my license. For the first time in over 3 years I was a licensed driver!

January, Dom told me she started seeing someone and she wasn't going to communicate with me anymore. Up to that point we were talking almost daily, and I would talk to Raya often too. It broke my heart! I shut down for two weeks didn't make calls, answered some, but wasn't in it, closed nothing. I binge watched the rest of True Blood- 40 hours in one week! It was the last remaining thing that wasn't finished or completed from my relationship with Dom. That's why I watched it the way I did, for completion. Then movies and more movies!

When I decided to get back to work it took 2 weeks to close anything. In January, I only earned $2,000.00. Better than nothing but not on track with my goals. My expenses were low, so I was still better off than I had been in years. All I had was phone bill, rent, and utilities. Low-stress living!

At the end of January, I had a meltdown! My legs were so sore from riding the bike anywhere I needed to go, I rode at least 6 days a week, I was sick of riding the bike, sick of not earning more, and pissed off I wasn't in a better place in life! I didn't leave my house for anything the last week of Jan. I just worked and watched movies. I did read the book Talk Like TED by Carmine Gallo. The science and studies cited in that book resonated deeply with me, my journey, and my pursuits. It really shed some light on a lot of the breaking points I've stumbled at or been able to push through. One of my favorite quotes to repeat to myself is, "You get what you tolerate" -Tony Robbins. So simple it has helped me improve my life repeatedly.

Chapter 22

I had a flight booked for Utah to go stay at the cabin for 10 days before flying to Eugene, Oregon for a logging expo we were running a booth at for our magazine. The 10 days at the cabin I made very few calls, spent all my time fixing my listings and putting them on new sites. I had a small deal close early in February and one closed the day we were flying to Oregon.

My rental car was a Dodge Challenger, my dream car! The fact that I was able to rent a car for myself meant so much to me, I was so grateful for the progress I was making in life! The show was awesome, it was amazing to see it all in person and gain appreciation for the machines I was selling! After it was it was all done, I stayed in Oregon a few days. I booked an air B&B on the coast.

Since it had been so long since I had driven, and I had the car I've wanted for years, I decided to just drive the coastal highway north! I decided I was going to see if I could get into Canada. I thought probably not because of my DUI and background, but they actually let me in! I spent the night in Vancouver, enjoyed great food and beautiful experiences as well as good life lessons.

When I got back to Savannah, I paid to have some work done on my scooter and have it shipped down to me. It took a couple of weeks to get it running right but once it was, I retired the bike and gave my legs a much-needed rest! I now had 8 horse power getting me where I wanted and needed to go! I even drove it all the way to the beach a few times! I was so happy to not have to pedal everywhere and to have a little more freedom!

My life consisted of the gym, work, movies, and going out to eat. Cold calling, listing equipment, pitching, closing. Send Bill of Sale and dealing with some pissed off customers on the occasion that a bad machine showed up. Having this happen is the worst! As an equipment broker, we do our best to make sure we're dealing with good credible sellers, sometimes we don't do good enough and it's horrible. It's a bad situation for the buyer and never feels good to be the one who relayed information to someone who trusted you to get it right and get them a good machine. It's very crippling and difficult to work through.

This job is a roller coaster! Sometimes 2-3 weeks without closing then earn $20k in two back to back $10k weeks! That was the 5-weeks leading up to the last two weeks of April for me. There were a lot of factors that contributed to that. It was my 6th month, a solid pipeline with a lot of equipment. Springtime working conditions making it time to buy!

I look back on it and the factor that stands out to me the most, me clarifying my vision. Having written down a clear picture of the apartment I was going to move into. Down to the small details of how I was going to decorate and especially what my bed was going to be and how it would look. I had been planning, preparing, and visualizing, but once I clearly wrote it out and then made every action I took directly tie to that vision, Boom! $20,581.00 month!

I'm glad I'm writing this out like this right now. It's helping me identify the fine/small details that make all the difference. Like, tying every action to that clear vision! When that is done, more energy comes to you and opportunities find you. Or we're finally taking enough action to truly see and capitalize on every opportunity! For me it's always a very spiritual experience!

Chapter 23

I traveled almost every month in early April 2018 to Utah to work the 1% Fitness booth at FitCon! Catch up with Rob and Tyson, and so I could spend some time with friends and family. All around a very successful trip. Although this was the first time in Utah that I didn't see Dom and Suraya. She had a new boyfriend again and cut communication. I was very resentful and had to do some AA step work with a friend to work through it. I was most upset that I had spoken to and made plans with Suraya right before communication was cut. But such is life. We just have to make the best of it all and learn as much as possible throughout!

Back to GA, gym, work, movies, restaurants. My gym goal was to be consistent 5-6 times a week no matter what. Some weeks it was only 4-times, but that was rare. I'd say 90% success rate for the year, very good! Especially considering I was traveling for expos and to track equipment or visit friends.

The goals were simple, find motivation in and of myself by myself for myself. Pay off debt, consistency at the gym, consistency with work. It was hard to stay motivated to work when I was sitting better financially than I ever had. It was easy to sleep in, work less, watch more movies, or go to the beach. The month of May, after my $20k month I called more than any other month, but I can look back and see I had no urgency and lost the shark mentality! Its explained best in the movie The Dark Knight Rises, "Peace has cost your strength, victory has defeated you." - Baine, one of my favorite movies because of the symbolism in it.

I remember waking up one morning, no alarm, 6:40am smiling ear to ear. I had been waking up and crushing my routine for 2 or more months straight! Up early, eating good, gym, work. $9k month, $13k month, $17k month! While sitting better financially than ever before! I was smiling because I found motivation in and of myself for myself by myself. The gym was daily no matter what regardless of where I was or what I was doing!

In October of 2018, I paid my last remaining payment to my dad! In the year of 2018 I paid off nearly $25k in debt and was beginning to rebuild my credit.

My work structure and discipline was and is locked in!

My dream car, the Dodge Challenger. My vision board shows a Hellcat, the jar describes the clarified vision of a Demon but that's future shit. I've been writing down that I would have a Dodge Challenger this year. My vision didn't stay clear, it was scrambled between 3 options. As the year went on and my written goals changed, I continually wrote that I would have a V8 6-speed manual transmission Dodge Challenger. I have it written down multiple times that Nov. 10th,

2018 I would be driving that car. I then made sure I spoke this out loud to the people in my life.

The few closest to me thought the date I chose was odd. I didn't realize until the day came that I chose a Saturday and it just so happened it was Veterans day that upcoming Monday, creating delays with the banks. I started the financing process Thursday the 8th, finalized Friday before end of business, the check was delayed until Tuesday the 13th. Regardless, I accepted delivery of my 2016 6 speed V8 Dodge Challenger Saturday Nov. 10th, 2018.

Of all the goals, the most difficult and longest one to accomplish was completing Og Mandino's, The Greatest Salesman in the World to the letter. Meaning, there are 10 scrolls that contain life-changing principals, and values. The prescribed manner to read them is: once, first thing in the morning in silence. Then after your mid-day meal in silence, and finally out loud before retiring at night. You are to repeat this for 30 continuous days without breaking the cycle for each scroll before advancing to the next. The 4th scroll, on the mourning (?)of my 13th reading I fell asleep before reading.

The second I woke up I knew I fucked up. I was furious, I wanted to proceed. My mind whispered, if you cheat, you're only cheating yourself. So, I started that scroll over from day one. That book taught me so much about life and discipline. That goal was the most difficult and longest I have ever accomplished. The prescribed manner is done so that the principals will lock into your subconscious and take hold of your daily actions and habits. It's a magical process to witness as the result of your consistent daily actions.

I've watched my work ethic increase and slack. I've learned from both. I've watched my structure and discipline stretch, flex and break. I've pushed myself to my limits. Blown up, screamed, yelled, and argued with those closest to me. Especially my boss and friend Chris Woods, my co-worker and friend Sam Wall and my best friend and future Olympic gold medalist Dominque Dulaney.

Those closest to me mentioned and not mentioned understand I push my limits to the point of explosion! With focus and effort to improve myself. To find the limit, push it, break it and expand! I respond and react better nowadays. I do better, understanding when to rest or calm instead of unnecessarily exploding. I've watched myself go on like that for months until I reach a new level of effort and ability. I have also learned to find the rest within the relentless push for improvement.

Being able to observe myself taking-action but in a slower more efficient manner, preserving energy for top priority tasks, and producing better results. Realizing I don't always have to go all out balls to the wall. I have experienced mental, physical, spiritual, and emotional changes and healing. Watching my body change its cravings and increase its sleep quality. Naturally set a cutoff time for caffeine and coffee. Become hypersensitive to supplements and medicines.

As I've progressed myself and my life spiritually, mentally, physically, and emotionally. Dissecting everything, diving into my soul, healing changing up-rooting. I've witnessed everything in and around me change. It shows through my external circumstances, my tone, posture, and mannerisms. With my financial situation improving to where it's not a stress, I've been blessed to be able to watch my spiritual state improve to the point that I can feel it sorting my mind and body out. Having muscle issues go away that have pained me for years. It's all been a result of trial and error process done with real time experiences.

I've watched my vices improve by studying my behaviors more closely. Indulging in vices food, sex, porn. Indulging with the purpose of understanding the core cause, embracing it so that I can grow my awareness of it and change it from the inside out.

I have tracked progress across the board! Of course, I have good days and I have bad days. Sometimes those bad days add up to a week, but I can honestly say with all the work I've done those bad days very rarely go longer than a week! We are all human, we all do our best and sometimes our best is kind of shitty. The good news is we all have the ability to improve and be less shitty and eventually really good. It simply takes effort and it's amazing how small the effort can be. If it's consistent it will eventually tip the scale. Once that happens, we have momentum to put a little more effort in and repeating this simple process daily just for today will overcome anything that stands in your way. Anything you want to improve on can be handled in this manner.

Chapter 24

December 26th, 2017, I had no license, was riding a pedal bike, and had over $25k in debt. I could ask people for help and always get it but not without being a huge stress and burden on those willing to help. Today Jan 29th, 2019, I got back from the first true vacation of my life, landing in Dublin and journeying all the way to the Shetland Islands of Scotland and back. I did anything and everything I wanted to. Made mistakes, was late to ferries, paid for quality. Bought nice things for myself and my family. Experienced cultures. Had great interactions with new exciting people. For two weeks with no phone and no GPS. Getting lost asking for directions and getting help, figuring things out on my own. Discovering beautiful structures and landscapes in foreign lands. I was able to do all this absolutely, stress-free, not even a thought about responding to any work.

I've practiced sales for more than 15 years now, no matter what my full time or part time job was, I was studying sales books, techniques, and processes. Working sales jobs for free or little pay. Attending sales workshops and seminars, fire walks etc. Doing sales role plays with anybody that was in sales and was willing. Knocking doors, collecting debts, running booths. Traveling just to sell. Studying the greats, bussing tables at night just to spend the days on a talented sales floor, just to watch and learn! Endured 13 months of selling credit card processing just for B2B experience!

The most I had ever earned in 12 months before was $65k. My goal for the 1st year with this job was $120k. In my first 12 months I earned $95,700.00 That's in my first 12 months in the industry. For the year of 2018, I Earned $106k. $14k shy of my goal which I am disappointed in only because I can look back and see holes in my work ethic that would have produced that amount. On the same token with that experience, growth, and determination, I know how to improve, do better, and earn more! My goal for 2019 is $250,000.00 in personal earning. Last January, I earned $2,000.00. This January, even after taking two weeks off, I earned $8,000.00.

My boss told me I'd take 2 weeks to get back to closing anything. I left a deal hanging in the air before I left that closed when I got back and closed 2 more deals on top of that. That's my Higher Power, The Universe rewarding my faith in, "taking the journey and preparing for a still greater journey" -Wallace D. Wattles Science of Getting Rich

I wrote earlier in this book of my desire and goal to move to Ireland. That my trip fell within my 3 to 5-year plan to move there. The day I returned to Savannah, I booked a flight to return to Ireland to spend more time there, see how realistic it is to work my current job from over there, and move there as close to that time frame as possible! Again, my every action, thought, sacrifice, and production is directly connected to moving to Ireland as soon as possible! It's ALL IN living and it's the best way we can live to ensure we get what our hearts desire!

Looking out the plane window while in Dublin, knowing I was leaving the place I want to be broke my heart! It made me cry, my mind was telling me to get off the plane. It was reaching for something to hold onto, to be able to stay. I was mad that I wasn't using my phone during the trip because if I would have, then I would have been working and had very few reasons to go back to Savannah. My mind reminded me about my car, my apartment, and my job. I didn't care about any of it in that moment, I just wanted to stay.

See when we're honest with ourselves, our hearts and emotions and feelings, we have an opportunity to take that powerful energy and fuel our pursuit! That's why the vision must be crystal clear. I've visualized my Alpaca Farm in Ireland for nearly 5 years now. I only spent 3 quick days in Ireland, but I confirmed in real life everything I've visualized is real and exactly how I've imagined. I've been there in mind.

The physical reality simply checked the box and put it into my heart! It all aligned, now I am magnetized to my reality, to my dream, my passion, purpose, and platform! I can't help myself, every single action is locked to that purpose and goal. It will be mine sooner than later! This is the truth because I've said so and I work my ass off relentlessly to make it so!

The image below is a dual image, the top being the picture on my wall in my bedroom that I stare at every night. The bottom image is a picture of the same cliff that I personally took.

This is the simple process. It takes practice and that's all. Daily practice big or small, doesn't matter, the only thing that matters is that it's daily. Visualize, clarify your vision to the smallest detail. Be grateful for everything "good" or "bad" in life because it's all for the better.

And believe, believe that you can achieve! That those achievements will eventually get you exactly what you want! You must find a way to believe with complete conviction that it's yours! Then work your ass off so you can capitalize on every opportunity! More importantly, show your gratitude and appreciation by taking full advantage of EVERY opportunity that comes your way!

Oh, and probably most important. Don't forget to thank your Higher Power! What or whoever that is. The Universe, Buddha, Allah, Jesus, God, Science, The Big Bang, Quanta, Wicca, The ALL, Greeks Gods, Pagan Gods. Nothing, Everything! Just give thanks for something outside yourself. If you look back on your entire life, it's hard to deny the existence of some outside force, isn't it?

Look, I sleep in and stay up late sometimes. I watch movies all day instead of work. I skip the gym, over-eat, and indulge in junk food. I spend stupidly sometimes. I can break a 2-month streak of not watching porn by deciding to give in all weekend. I sometimes yell at people and can be an asshole. There are times that I try to help and fuck things up worse, or I do my best to do good business, miss the standard, and it ends up being bad business. I'm human and experience the same emotions and feelings as everyone else. I have vices and virtues.

Somedays I feel like I'm in control and other days I feel like I've never had a clue what control is. I battle my mind, my fears, and insecurities. Rack my brain wondering why I can be so confident in some areas and completely lack confidence in others. I have doubts and I am constantly pushing to live in a way that overcomes our human condition by having a clear and simplified focus and a definite purpose.

I am able to overcome all of these oppositions. It's not easy. I am able to work through heartbreaks and seeming failure. I can find more energy to push past tired, exhausted, and sick. I find the ability to overcome the emotions and the tricks of the mind. It's all still there, it's just as real as it is for everybody else. It's simply disregarded and accepted as an usher to success guiding me through doors to bigger, better, bolder pursuits!

This conviction has only come through self-taught knowledge, practice, trial and error, and conversations with those doing the same. The books I've mentioned in this book are books I've listened to or read repeatedly. The more books I read, the more often I came across the same studies being cited. The same proofs, themes, principals and philosophies. Tracing them back to the ancient wisdom in the books, "As A Man Thinketh," "The Greatest Salesman in the World," "Science of Getting Rich," at this point these are my 3 go-to's. There are many that have helped me and again it's been very important for me to see the common studies and themes across 100's of books.

This is where I leave you, to draw what conclusions you will and let your mind run where it may.

"Most people overestimate what they can do in a year and they underestimate what they can do in two or three decades." -Tony Robbins

5-year prophecy! Feb. 2023

o Own/operate Royalpaca Farm in Ireland, over-looking the Cliffs of Moher, sitting on 10 acres with a 3 bed 3.5 bath cobblestone house and a 3 car garage. Own 60 alpaca, well rights, barn, lean-to, a fiber mill, wool processing/cleaning shed, and a sewing/design warehouse. I create my own designs from start to finish, all original and handmade. Royalpaca is all profitable with steady sales increases quarterly and markets expanding to all global cold climate areas.

- Release my second GHOSTLYFE book, self-published, circulating Amazon, kindle, and making its way, along with my first book, into Barnes & Noble with a large marketing display in every store to promote it!

- GHOSTLYFE is gaining recognition worldwide, I am speaking to large audiences and being invited to speak on top rated tv, radio, and podcasts
- $10.6 million in profitable assets and cash flow
- Own my Demon Dodge Challenger, flat black, completely murdered out, with a classic GHOSTLYFE symbol, diagonal across the hood

Made in the USA
Columbia, SC
25 March 2019